HOW DO THEY DO IT?

◆ ◆ ◆

Penthouse lovers share their passion in every conceivable combination . . . as bedroom intimates taking a new and thrillingly unexpected position . . . as erotic adventurers finding love with the improper stranger . . . or as carnal gourmands plunging into joyful couplings of three, or even more. Where do they do it? At home or on the highway . . . by the pool or at the casino . . . amid the cacophony of the big city or the isolation of the wilderness . . . wherever opportunity and their active libidos will take them. They're about to take you with them. And all you've got to do is be ready.

◆ ◆ ◆

OTHER BOOKS IN THE SERIES:

More Letters from Penthouse
Erotica from Penthouse
Letters to Penthouse III
Letters to Penthouse IV

**Published by
WARNER BOOKS**

ATTENTION: SCHOOLS AND CORPORATIONS
WARNER books are available at quantity discounts with bulk purchase for educational, business, or sales promotional use. For information, please write to: SPECIAL SALES DEPARTMENT, WARNER BOOKS, 1271 AVENUE OF THE AMERICAS, NEW YORK, N.Y. 10020

EROTICA FROM PENTHOUSE III

THE EDITORS OF PENTHOUSE MAGAZINE

WARNER BOOKS

A Time Warner Company

Penthouse® is a registered trademark of Penthouse International, Limited.

Enjoy lively book discussions online with CompuServe. To become a member of CompuServe call 1-800-848-8199 and ask for the Time Warner Trade Publishing forum. (Current members GO:TWEP.)

If you purchase this book without a cover you should be aware that this book may have been stolen property and reported as "unsold and destroyed" to the publisher. In such case neither the author nor the publisher has received any payment for this "stripped book."

WARNER BOOKS EDITION

Copyright © 1994 by Penthouse International, Limited
All rights reserved.

Cover design by Don Puckey

Warner Books, Inc.
1271 Avenue of the Americas
New York, NY 10020

**Visit our Web site at
http://warnerbooks.com**

A Time Warner Company

Printed in the United States of America

First Printing: December, 1994

10 9 8 7 6 5

CONTENTS

Fill 'Er Up	1
Humpin' Jack Flash	7
Italian Stallion	10
Backseat Driver	13
Wheels of Fortune	16
The Night Is Young	21
Mr. Fix-It	27
Screen Testes	34
The Cockteaser and the Screaming Prick	41
Hot Rods and Rubber Dolls	49
Working Late	52
The Couple and the Bachelor	58
The Gift of Tongues	72
Private Showing	78
Trivial Pursuit	85
The Best Medicine	92
Clean and Supple	96
Overexposed	100
In Concert	108
Test Flight	113
Ride 'Em	118
Wives on the Waves	124
Heart & Soul	128
Office Orientation	132
Strip Trip	141
French Girl	145
A Soldier's Story	156
Beth and the Frat Boy	162
Bahamas Getaway	170
Box Lunch	176
Wild Strawberries	181

Dutch Treat	184
All Hands on Deck	191
A Girl Called Spike	200
More Than a Mouthful	205
The Widow Maker	210

Short, sweet and to the point ... of climax. The stories contained in this volume are of the no-frills, no-holds-barred variety. They're graphic, sexy, surprising, uncensored. So take some clothes off and dive right in. These stripped-down tales of lust leave little to the imagination. It's all here.

John Borrelli
Managing Editor
Penthouse Special Publications

Fill 'er Up

I was driving along Highway 61 toward New Orleans and noticed the fuel gauge was near empty, so I took the next exit and drove into the first service station I saw. It was in a place called Gramercy. After I filled the tank, I ran into the office to pay the bill and started running back when—wham!—I bumped into a woman who was bending over, tapping the wheel-bolt covers of a van with her fist. I put both my hands on her shoulders so she wouldn't fall.

"Terribly sorry," I apologized. "I'm late for New Orleans and didn't notice . . ." But then I did notice—and I stopped breathing and stared openmouthed. She was the most gorgeous, stunningly perfect redhead I'd ever seen or ever will see. Titian tresses cascaded over bare shoulders, framing lustrous eyes that spoke to me, although the sounds she made emerged from delicately formed crimson lips. Her modulated drawl told me she wasn't from the Deep South.

"I'm unhurt, really," she said, "so if you'd stop squeezing my shoulders . . ."

That shock of beholding such beauty had left me frozen in position, nearly speechless.

"Excuse me," I blurted. "I was afraid you might have

fallen. Pavement could have scratched you. My clumsiness is inexcusable. May I help? Trouble with wheel covers?"

My bursts of tongue-tied speech seemed to amuse her as she smiled forgivingly.

"Well, I lost one a while ago, so now I check them a couple of times a day. If you're in a rush to get to New Orleans, don't waste your time."

She said it so pleasantly that I knew I couldn't let this glory-of-creation go.

"I was in a hurry only because I'm hungry. Know any good restaurants in the city?"

"New Orleans? Too many to mention. What kind of food do you like?"

"Whatever you prefer," I replied, trying not to sound flippant. "That is, if you'll dine with me."

It seemed an eternity before she smiled brightly and said, "I thought you'd never ask. I'm really tired of cooking in my van. My name's Teri."

"And I'm Pat."

We arranged that I'd follow Teri to the outskirts of New Orleans, where she'd park the van and ride with me in my car to the Latin Quarter. She knew of a really good restaurant there in a quaint old hotel. When we reached the suburbs she parked at a huge shopping mall. I waited while she locked the van. As she approached my car, her slit skirt revealing her shapely legs, I jumped out to open the door for her. The sight of her seated in my Honda almost overpowered me.

"You like my legs?" she asked directly as I climbed back into the driver's seat.

"Didn't think I was that obvious," I said. "Yes, they're peerless. Hope you don't mind. Afraid I've been staring. Just can't control myself."

"I'm glad. You're not so bad, either. Why isn't your wife with you?"

Although I knew it might end things too soon, I had to be truthful. "The final decree is due in eighteen days."

Looking at me with a radiant smile, she slid over close and placed her hand on my crotch, stroking me there lightly.

"You're a few months behind me as a divorcé. I know how hard the waiting can be. You must be starved for more than food by now. Have many girlfriends?"

Her deft fingers unzipped my fly and moved over my stiffening tool.

"Wow! That's bigger than I hoped! Let's see if it gets any bigger!" She continued stroking gently and it began growing. "Oh Pat! It does get bigger! What a man! Wow, I'm glad we met. I want it! Let's do it before dinner. The hotel's on the next block. Park in the hotel's garage so we can register and go right up to our room."

I did as she suggested. In the garage I had to fight back an urge to slip her dress up her lovely thighs as soon as we parked. I did slide my hand under her dress, however. She opened her legs and I felt her soft crotch, massaging it until it turned moist. The garage was dimly lit, and I considered screwing her in the car. No, I decided, Teri was too classy for that action. Just then she zipped up my fly and looked at me with a lovely expectant smile. We quickly registered and went to our room, where I immediately lost all control. I pulled her into a tight embrace. Pressing my open mouth to hers, I dropped my pants and raised her skirt.

"Unzip the back," she breathed. When her skirt fell, skimpy blue underpants were revealed to my hungry eyes. I led her over to the bed and at the same time removed her blouse. After throwing off all my clothes, I slowly undid her bra clasp, revealing firm, full breasts and erect, crimson nipples. Bending forward to kiss each one, then to suck and stroke them, I was lost in passion. Teri rubbed her crotch against my leg and then let her tight bikinis drop to the floor.

She stood on tiptoe and raised her splendid ass slightly above my stiff cock. Then she slowly lowered her pussy toward my standing rod. It was wonderfully tight as it met my cockhead. After resisting penetration for a second or two, it suddenly opened and slid completely over the top of my engorged cock.

"Oh God," Teri gasped. "That feels good! Oh Pat, I knew we'd fit! Oh, push hard!"

I moved my prick in and out, withdrawing it momentarily now and then to roll the head against her clit. Teri was breathing in husky, ecstatic gasps. After I-don't-know-how-long, she pulled me with her to the bed's edge and sat there with her snatch pressed forward against my thrusts. We fit so tightly and held on so ardently that my rod stayed in her while we moved from one position to another.

As we screwed face-to-face in a sitting position, Teri leaned back slightly, her rosy breasts and erect nipples exciting me beyond belief. I pumped in and out like a ramrod, resisting orgasm until Teri was ready. When she suddenly shouted "Fuck me, honey!" I removed my cock, pressed her back on the bed and, as her legs spread wide, I jammed my throbbing cock as deep as it could go into her. Her cunt muscles were coaxing me to a frenzy, but I held on, driving in and out till I nearly burst. Suddenly her moans were louder. "Oh Pat! . . . You're really fucking me now! . . . Don't stop!"

My dick squirted violently just as her juices began squishing forth. I pumped her completely full. Then I squirted out more, so that my thick fluid was forced back between my cock and her snatch before it dribbled down her legs. It was a glorious climax! I couldn't seem to stop coming—and I didn't want to. Neither did Teri, who continued fucking herself on my throbbing dick. Gradually we slowed down, and my rod gave one last little squirt. I dropped my open mouth on hers for a loving, grateful kiss. "I hope you feel as good as I do," I whispered, hoping the moment would linger.

"I've never been fucked this well before. Where did you learn how to please a woman so completely?"

"Didn't have to learn. With you, making love comes naturally."

We kissed noisily, openmouthed, with my cock still pulsing gently within her. Then, somehow, I knew she wanted to wash up. I carried her to the shower. As she stepped in, I couldn't quit staring at her glorious nakedness. I scrubbed her back first, then her graceful ass, and then I washed between her pussy lips very gently, rinsing away my semen. This turned her on again. She took my hands, placed them over her snatch and backed into me. My cock plunged right into her snatch. She grabbed it and worked it all the way into her tight pussy. We began fucking immediately, right there in the shower, with Teri bent forward so that my short strokes rubbed her clit. She soon reached back around my rump and pulled me against her so that my dick reached farther into her. On each of my backstrokes, she would shove it in deep again. She began to moan in cadence with my excited, hard breathing—I knew we were nearing another crescendo.

"Oh Pat! You're giving it to me good! Fuck me! *Fuck* me!"

This time, again, we were right on. Her juices flowed copiously as my come squirted up her cunt. My cock pulsated wildly, gushing an immense load while she fucked back in full joy. Once again rolls of thick creamy fluid rolled down her legs, only this time the shower washed it right away. I kept squeezing my prick into her until the squirting slowed to a last happy spurt. I didn't want to let go, but she removed her hands from my rump and turned to give me a wet, noisy kiss.

Suddenly she dropped down and kissed my still-throbbing

rod. "Pat, I've never sucked anyone, not even my ex. That's one reason he and I broke up. If you'd like, though, I'll suck you off." Her heavenly face was looking up at me, and I could do only one thing. I lifted her up and kissed her everywhere—her lovely breasts, tits, navel, her dimpled ass, her mound—but I didn't stick my tongue in her cunt. I'd never liked the idea of oral sex. Apparently, she didn't like it, either.

"There's only one place for your lovely lips." I said, and I kissed her endlessly.

"Pat, I've got to tell you that I saw you drive into the station and I stalled around. When you bumped into me, I know it was accidental, but I was glad for the chance to talk. I knew we'd hit it off."

So it began. Teri and I drove to Miami after she returned the rented van. We stayed together while I worked across the USA, fucking together several times every night. Then, in Seattle, an argument arose from a minor difference of opinion and Teri stormed out of the hotel. I saw my stupidity in seconds and ran after her, but she had vanished. I searched all night and even hired a private detective, but to no avail.

Just a couple of weeks ago I saw a van crossing the border, headed for Vancouver, while I was crossing south to Seattle. For sure it was Teri at the wheel. By the time I'd turned around and got back through Canadian customs, she'd vanished again.

Humpin' Jack Flash

My marriage and sex life with Laurie was satisfactory, but becoming more and more routine. Swinging was out because she couldn't accept my dorking anyone else. So was a ménage. "No bitch is going to eat my cunt," she said. "Another man, maybe."

That was food for fantasy! Seeing Laurie's beautiful pussy impaled, or seeing a big, blue-veined cock in her mouth—yeah, I could go for that! Unfortunately, she claimed she could never do it in my presence or with my knowledge. Since secrecy is too much like cheating, we found ourselves at an impasse. But a fire was lit!

Laurie and I center our social life around a private club. Besides the live music and camaraderie, there is plenty of pot smoking in the parking lot. Many of our friends would love to get in Laurie's panties. Some would come in their pants if they knew we often fantasize about them.

Fantasy was all it was for a long while. Then one day my friend Jack and I stepped outside to share a joint. Jack played drums with the band, but he was also a photographer. When I saw that his van was loaded with photography equipment, my mind went clickety-click! Laurie and I had fooled around with cameras, trying to take pictures of ourselves fucking and sucking, and I knew she got off on it.

After the next dance set, Laurie and I invited Jack out for a little herb. Naturally the conversation turned to photography and our lack of success at it. He took the bait and asked, "Wanna use my equipment?"

"Naw," I replied. "I can't take decent pictures. Why don't you take them?"

"Jim, are you crazy?" Laurie protested, but with a sparkle in her eye that wasn't from the cannabis.

Back inside, she asked if I'd been serious. "Hell yes!" I said. "What's it going to hurt if he looks?" Best ease into it slowly, I knew, but I also knew if she ever let Jack get that far, she'd probably get fucked by him.

After the club closed that night, the three of us hopped into the van and headed for the beach. Laurie was nervous. She said she wanted to change from her dress and high heels. Under her dress she was wearing nothing but a garter belt and long hose.

Our moonlight session began tamely. But we were already on a roller coaster with but one way to go, and Laurie soon consented to pose for some titty shots—and she's really got a pair of melons, size 36C with silver-dollar nipples. A bit more coaxing convinced Laurie to hike up her dress, exposing her black bush. More cajoling from me and her knees parted. Jack set up a battery-powered spotlight that found her pussy lips engorged and dripping. Very little effort was required to get her naked—and no effort at all to get her to masturbate for the camera.

I nixed Jack's suggestion that I fuck Laurie while he got it on film. "No," I said. "Let me take the pictures. You fuck her." Laurie's eyes popped open when she heard this, but she never missed a stroke on her clit.

Jack's cock is bigger than mine, but I was too wound up

for jealousy. Using a zoom lens, I got to within inches of her gaping pussy being filled by his thick shaft. I snapped several shots of her humping her crotch to meet and take it all! Incredible! I soon laid the camera down, however. I was too horny for any more picture-taking. I needed release and considered beating off.

Then I thought about Laurie's mouth. She and Jack were going at it missionary-style, and she took my meat in her mouth like a wild animal. Humping, grinding, twisting, turning, her gyrations caused my dick to slip out and I was shocked when Jack immediately engulfed it in his mouth. No way could I back out as he sucked it all the way in and greedily swallowed the quart of come I couldn't hold back when he and Laurie reached tremendous climaxes.

Jack and I switched places after a brief rest. Fucking Laurie while she slurped and deep-throated his rod was fantastic. Before it was over, though, she held his one-eyed monster up to my face. I sure hope that sucking one dick doesn't make you a real cocksucker!

Italian Stallion

My name is Scott and I'm a horny twenty-year-old Italian who loves to eat pussy! I'm about five feet ten inches tall and weigh about one hundred sixty pounds. I have piercing blue eyes and light brown hair. I've always done more than all right with the ladies and, up till recently, I honestly considered myself God's gift to the fairer sex.

Fran is about five feet seven inches tall with beautiful blonde hair and sensuously arousing big brown eyes! She weighs about one hundred fifteen pounds and she's got a body that won't quit! She's a perfect "10"! I usually go for gorgeous blondes with blue eyes, but in Fran's case I made an exception, as who wouldn't after seeing her tantalizing walk and tasting her kiss of death (so to speak)?

It all started one rainy afternoon at her log cabin in Pennsylvania. I asked her if she'd ever had a back rub and, to my surprise, she said no—adding that she'd like to see what it was like. The reason for my surprise was that she had been married for seven years (now, at the age of twenty-five, she's a widow). I jumped at the opportunity to show her what she'd been missing for all these years. Having wanted to make it with her since first laying eyes on her, the mere thought of just touching this chick had my balls in an uproar! I knew that within the hour I'd be engaged in the hottest sexual encounter I could ever imagine!

I recalled a bit of advice from my favorite Italian uncle, Joe, who told me, "Always remember, Scotty, you gotta kiss it first." When Uncle Joe's words crossed my mind I envisioned Fran's hot cunt pouring pussy cream into the depths of my throat and I began foaming at the mouth.

During her first back rub, I could sense that Fran was really getting turned on when I "accidentally on purpose" fondled her hard, erect nipples. As my hands slid up along her shirt, she let out squeals of sheer excitement. Then I whispered into her ear that I wanted nothing more than to lick her sweet pussy. I remember telling her that she reminded me of a beautiful genie and asking her if I could make a wish. "Anything, master," she replied breathlessly. "Anything at all!"

The first wish popped into my mind. "I wish your skirt would disappear along with your shirt, leaving you with nothing on except your panties," I said. Her reply was, "Your every wish is my command."

God, was I hard at the sight of her translucent white bloomers! All I could think of was burying my face in that soft blonde bush of my newfound genie's. Next she pleaded, "Make another wish, master," and all I could think of was for her to spread her legs and beg me to kiss her pussy. She readily obliged, saying, "Kiss it, master. Drink my come, master. Oh, master, please drink my come."

By now I couldn't resist anymore. I had to have her! I tore her undies from her hot pleading thighs and went down on her. Kissing her inner thighs, I found pussy juice already streaming down them. I became aware of her delicate and irresistible feminine odor as I then dove into her golden-hued muff and quickly found her throbbing love-button!

Fran begged me to show her what us Italian guys are all

about, and you can bet I did. Driven by pure passion and lust, I grabbed her by her hips with both hands and thrust my pointed tongue deep into her burning cunt! She bucked and screamed at the top of her lungs as I worked my tongue in and out of her. My Dago nose was bumping against her clit in rhythm to the song coming from the radio, "Too Fast for Love" by Motley Crüe!

We never did make it to the bedroom, but when I told her that she should make a wish, she said, "Fuck me, master! Come in me!" I felt I owed it to her, so right there on the floor, I climbed aboard and shot the mother load deep inside her. All I can say now is that our two-and-one-half-month-old son must have gotten his looks from his mom. He's already a little stud and, with his blond hair and blue eyes, I know he's gonna be capable of driving women wild!

Backseat Driver

I was eighteen and so was she. I had loved her since eighth grade. We lived in a small town in the hills of northern Minnesota.

I loved her from a distance, without sexual overtones, until one hot summer day. Then, one day in July, she was walking down Main Street with a friend as I came out of the drugstore. I think my heart stopped as I stood spellbound, watching her. She had the most beautiful tan I'd ever seen. She was wearing black shorts and a white halter. As she walked by and out of sight, I felt the first true stirring of desire in my loins. This was the first time I'd felt any great need to have sex with a woman.

From that day forward, my love for her was accented by a burning sexual desire, which I did not fully understand. Virtually every night I masturbated while fantasizing about her and her beautiful black shorts.

It was later in our senior year before we ever dated. I was always too shy to ask her out. She had been going with the "rich kid" in town since she was a freshman. I'd remained a virgin. Athletics and schoolwork had dominated my time, for I hoped to earn a scholarship to a major university.

Through it all, though, my total and burning love for her never waned.

Then, in December, at a school dance, she came up to me and said, "Aren't you ever going to ask me out?" I was very embarrassed and mumbled something stupid. She took my hand and said, "Come on, let's dance." The band was playing a medley of slow pieces and, as we danced, I felt my cock rising against my zipper. I almost died of embarrassment when my swollen member brushed against her leg every now and then. Slowly she began to press her beautiful, slender body against me until my erection was impressed against her abdomen. The ballroom (actually our school gym) seemed almost nonexistent to me. All I could think about was her sexy body and the sensations awakening in my cock. I heard my voice saying, "I love you," and I heard her repeat the words after me.

I'm not certain how we got there, but we were soon in the backseat of my '57 Ford, frantically feeling each other's body and kissing without letup.

She wasn't very experienced but knew far more than I did. She became a playful leader while I did little more than writhe and moan in anticipation. She undid her blouse and bra and her small, white, beautiful jutting breasts were suddenly mine to see. They were delicately traced with what remained of her summer tan. My breath came in uneven gasps as she pulled my face to them. I heard myself uttering the word "fuck" as I nibbled, licked and sucked her hardened nipples. She laughed gleefully and said, "Let's take off our clothes."

The sight of her naked body was almost more than I could bear. She was beautiful beyond my hottest dream of her. The whiteness of her lower belly contrasted sharply with the large V of soft, dark, curly hair below. My cock was so hard as I gawked at her naked body that I thought it would break. She softly touched the end of it and said, "You're losing your oil." Looking away from her pussy for a moment, I saw the droplets of pre-come falling one by one from the tip of my throbbing cock.

She slowly lay down on the seat and spread her legs so that I could see the pink between her pussy lips as they parted for me. She gently pulled me onto her and, as I swung one of my legs over her, my cock rubbed against her thigh. Immediately I started squirting come all over her legs and stomach. I gasped and moaned in ecstasy as my cock released all my pent-up desire. Before I finished coming, she placed my cock into her sweet pussy and I felt like the world could end at that moment without any regrets on my part.

I came twice more before pulling my cock from her lovenest. We kissed and talked for hours afterward and I managed two more orgasms, perhaps more aptly described as two painful spasms from an aching but lustful and quite empty cock.

Wheels of Fortune

I'm in my early twenties, stand five feet eleven inches tall, and have a muscular build, which is lucky for without it I would never have survived that strenuous and exciting night. It started at a party. Since most of my friends were working or out of town, I figured I'd have to go by myself and just play wallflower. Boy, was I wrong! Some people that I knew showed up, and before long, we were knee-deep in a drinking game. The game was going into extra innings when I decided I'd better cool it since I had to drive home. So I got up and literally ran into a girl I'd known in high school. We started talking, but it became increasingly harder to hear what she was saying as the party grew livelier. She suggested we go for a walk. We did, and it was really pleasant, but it ended far too soon—before I'd had a chance to do anything. In hopes it would lead somewhere, I offered her a ride to her dorm. I parked my cycle in the lot behind the building, where she got off and started to go, then abruptly turned around and came back to push me gently onto my motorcycle seat. While I sat there stunned, she knelt quickly between my legs, unzipped my fly, and pulled out my quickly hardening cock.

"I can never resist a gentleman," she said, more to my

throbbing dick than to me, before she kissed it lightly. Her lips were so soft and caressing as she slowly slid her mouth up and down my manhood, her warm tongue lapping from the base all the way to the head of my dick. It wasn't long before I sent my come shooting down her hungry throat, while I stifled my moans and grunts in my hands. As carefully as she could, she slipped my dick back into my pants and zipped me up. When she stood up, she ran her tongue over her lips and captured an escaping drop of come from the corner of her mouth so seductively that I was instantly hard again. She gave me a peck on the cheek and hurried off. As I stood there stunned but satisfied, I heard someone clapping behind me. I laughed to myself and got the hell out of there to return to the party. The night was still young and I badly needed a drink.

I was just getting off my cycle when I saw that my roommate had joined the party. He was talking with a blonde who displayed a very full set of breasts and a beautiful round ass. I said, "Hello," and she smiled. When she saw my helmet in my hand, her smile evolved from friendly into excited rather quickly. She immediately asked if she could go for a ride, and who am I to refuse such a request?

I drove her around the neighborhood for a while, going fast enough to make her clutch my waist and press her warm, firm breasts against my back. Looking for a place where we could be alone, I parked in a dark schoolyard and asked her if she would like to check the place out. She quickly agreed as we walked into the shadows. Within a second I had covered her fabulous tits with my hands and pressed my lips against hers in a passionate kiss. Moving my hands across her flat stomach to her crotch, I caressed her wet pussy through her jeans, making her breathe faster and more heavily. I was kissing her neck and ear when she whispered rather forcefully into my ear that she wanted me to take my pants down right then because she wanted to do it. Again, who am I to argue? Moving deeper into the shadows, I yanked my pants to my ankles and eagerly sat down on the steps, while she hurriedly removed her pants and dripping panties. She nearly jumped on top of my rock-hard cock, and before I could catch my breath, she was rocking back and forth so hard that I thought she was going to rip my dick off. Just as I was falling in time with her rhythm, she started to buck and moan and scream in the throes of passion. Suddenly a car's headlights flashed over us. She gathered her senses and as fast as she had taken her clothes off, she just stepped back into them, leaving me sitting there with my pole waving in the breeze. I reluctantly put my clothes on and drove her back to the party, where she thanked me and disappeared into the house.

Feeling frustrated, I walked into the house and ran into the hostess of the party, a girl I had been seeing on again and off again for the past several months. Lynn asked if we could go somewhere private to talk. After twenty minutes of riding through the deserted streets, we came to a desolate part of town. I parked the cycle, wondering what she would do this time. She didn't disappoint me. As always happens when she drinks and rides a motorcycle, she was hornier than hell. No sooner had I stepped off my bike than she had wrapped one arm around my waist and was desperately massaging my cock through my pants with her other hand. Not willing to be left out, I quickly began massaging her soft, ample tits and pulling her shirt and bra up around her shoulders. I flicked my tongue teasingly around her swollen nipples, which usually drives her crazy. She was getting so worked up that she could barely talk without gasping for breath, and I wasn't all that steady either, especially with her hand inside my pants fervently pulling and stroking my cock. So we both zipped up and straightened up before racing back to her house.

When we got there, the party had died down considerably,

and she led me rather sternly through what was left of the crowd to her bedroom. Once the door was shut, she quickly helped me remove my clothes, then slowly and seductively stripped off her own. Totally naked, she playfully leapt onto her water bed with her legs spread wide and her head thrown back. Taking my cue, I eased between her legs and slowly kissed and nipped my way from her toes up her long, luscious legs. Licking teasingly around her steaming cunt, I continued to her navel, which I tickled with my tongue, making her laugh. Then I trailed my tongue across her stomach, leaving traces of hot, hungry saliva, and ascended to her breasts, which were heaving with excitement. I kissed her more forcefully around her nipples, up to her earlobes and back down to her right nipple, which I suddenly sucked into my mouth, making her gasp with pleasure.

Just when I sensed she was on the verge of coming, I stopped and slowly trailed kisses to her pouting cunt lips. I sucked on one lip, pulling gently before moving to the other, then plunged my tongue deep within her pussy. Her body tightened as I fucked her with my tongue, brought her to the edge of another orgasm, and then stopped again, lightly kissing her clit as she cooled down. When she was calm enough, I started sucking her clit and playing with her nipples with both hands. This time I didn't stop. I sucked and nipped and licked her clit until she wrapped her legs so tightly around my head that I could hardly breathe. Finally, with a trailing scream, she came. Her sweet wetness had only partly quenched my thirst.

Prying my head from the vise grip of her legs, I quickly shoved my cock as deeply as possible into her still-quivering cunt. Lynn instantly dug her fingertips into my back and shoulders as I pumped away, bringing her just to the brink, then easing away until she screamed for me to fuck her and not stop. That I did. I fucked her until I felt my balls tighten and shoot my hot load deep within her pulsating, gripping pussy. We collapsed for a short rest before feasting on the second course and the third and the fourth. . . .

I don't quite understand the magic appeal of motorcycles for some girls, but the two go together well enough to convince me that I'm never selling my bike.

The Night Is Young

I'm in my mid-forties, with a Dolly Parton figure (though I am a flaming redhead) which I'm very proud of. I still get admiring glances from men of all ages.

One weekend last summer, my son asked if he could bring his college roommate home to spend the weekend. I said sure and when they showed up, I was sitting by the pool in my bikini.

As Mike, the roommate, was introduced, his eyes roamed unashamedly over my body and I blushed in mingled embarrassment and pleasure that this young man was so obviously attracted to me. I suggested that they join me by the pool, and when they returned I could see that Mike was a fine specimen of young manhood. He had a body like Michelangelo's David, as perfectly proportioned as a Greek god, and there was a bulge in his swimsuit that left no doubt that he was very well-endowed.

I couldn't take my eyes off Mike's body as he dived into the pool and swam around. I must admit that my son's roommate had begun to inspire some very naughty thoughts in my mind.

After the swim, my son announced that he had a date and

would be out late. He invited Mike along and said he could get an extra girl, but Mike said he was tired and had some studying to do for a summer course he was taking. He'd just stay here this evening and cram if I didn't mind, he added. I noticed the emphasis he put on the word "cram," and it made me tingle in anticipation.

Since my husband was out of town on business, Mike and I were left alone that evening. It was a warm night, and I didn't bother to change out of my bikini. Also, to be honest, I was really getting turned on by Mike's obvious interest in my body and wanted him to keep getting a good look at everything I had.

I made some dinner and we discussed Mike's schoolwork. He was a varsity track-and-field man and had won a number of events. I couldn't resist asking him if he had a girlfriend. Mike just smiled and asked me if I really wanted to hear the whole story. I felt I might be taking this a bit too far but was too curious to resist, so I said yes.

Then Mike began to describe in graphic detail his quite numerous and really torrid sexual experiences with coeds and older women, too. He said he really liked older women, that they were infinitely superior to their younger sisters. This young stud had really been around!

He talked for over an hour, and I began to get horny as hell. He was really good at describing sex, and I felt my pussy getting wet.

Suddenly, without warning, he came over, put his arms around me and gave me a long soul kiss as he fumbled with my bikini top and then began to fondle my nipples.

I was hot as hell but realized this had gone far enough and began gently to push him away. His hand then dived into my bikini panties and his fingers found my clit. I have a clit the size of the tip of my little finger and it is incredibly sensitive. In the state I was in, his touch was like an electric shock. I moaned in pleasure and felt all my inhibitions vanish. Mike then kissed me, lifted me in his arms and carried me into the bedroom.

As he laid me on the bed, he was already pulling off my bikini panties. I was too far gone with frenzied lust to do anything more than mumble a feeble assent as he dived between my legs and began to eat me. He tongued my clit in an expert manner and brought me to a shattering orgasm almost immediately.

As I lay back panting, Mike dropped his trunks and revealed his monster meat—it was at least nine inches long, as thick as my wrist, with a beautiful upward curve. I'd never seen anything so magnificent—or as appealing.

Before I had a chance to say a word, he had raised my legs above my shoulders and inserted just the tip in my dripping pussy.

He slowly began to pump just the head of his cock in and out of my pussy. It was driving me crazy—I ached to have the whole thing inside me.

Finally, I could bear it no longer and asked him to shove it in all the way. Mike just smiled and told me to tell him how much I wanted him to fuck me. The bastard knew how much I wanted him and was going to tease me, but I needed him so badly I went along with his game.

Soon I began to get crazy with lust and begged him to fuck me. In one great thrust, Mike rammed his monster in me up to the hilt and then just held it there as I began frantically to squirm, begging him to screw me. As I came to a fantastic orgasm, he began pounding away for all he was worth and soon I could feel his cock spasm as he shot load after load in my love-box.

We just lay there for a while. Then Mike began slowly to ream out my aching cunt. He was still hard as a rock and he asked me if I would like him to frig my clit. I moaned my consent as he turned me over and slowly inserted himself, inch by inch, back into my willing pussy while he expertly fingered my clit. Soon I was heaving back against him as I approached another climax and his monster began to penetrate all the way into my cunt. We came almost at the same time in an incredible burst of ecstasy.

We had been fucking for nearly two hours and both needed a break, so I mixed some martinis as Mike took a shower. While Mike was in the bathroom, my son called and said he was spending the night with his girlfriend and wouldn't be home until the next afternoon. I told him that was just fine and joined Mike in the shower to tell him the good news. We couldn't keep our hands off each other in the shower, and after washing each other off and drying, we adjourned to the living room. Mike put his arm around me on the couch as, totally nude, we sipped our martinis. Mike asked if I had any good videos and I blushed since my husband had quite a collection and I really got turned on watching them. I asked him what kind he liked and he said orgy scenes.

I felt honestly embarrassed even though this young stud had just had me every which way, because I get terribly turned on by orgy videos. And I've always had a constant fantasy about trying it out some day. I brought a stack and asked Mike to take his pick. He selected one where Vanessa del Rio takes on half a dozen guys, one of my favorites though I didn't tell him so.

As the action got hotter, Mike's hands roamed over my body, getting me hot again as we watched Vanessa getting it from three guys at once.

Mike began to tell me about his experiences, describing the studs he said he could get me anytime I wanted. I went absolutely wild again, losing all control, and was soon on my knees sucking his meat for all I was worth. He shot another tremendous load down my throat and I eagerly squeezed him dry and licked his beautiful cock clean.

We were soon in bed again doing a fabulous 69 until I could stand it no longer and got on top of Mike. I rode him like a bronco while rubbing myself off to another great orgasm. Then I collapsed, exhausted. I had never had more than two orgasms with my husband and he never got it off more than twice with me. As I fell asleep with Mike's arms around me, I knew this would not be the last time I saw Mike. I knew I'd want him again and again.

During the night I woke up to find Mike on top of me, slowly rubbing the tip of his cock on my pussy lips. I asked him how long I had been asleep while he was caressing me and he said he'd just started. I reached down and squeezed the tip of his cock and felt wet, sticky fluid. I raised my fingers to my lips and licked them off. It was my own pussy juice! Somehow, this turned me on incredibly and Mike lowered himself to my pussy and began eating me out again, licking up my juices. When his tongue began to work over my clit I knew I was headed for another incredible climax and began to beg him to get me more young studs. I went crazy again and a torrent of obscenities poured from my lips as Mike mounted me again and shot his fourth load in my cunt, all the while telling me how I was going to love having half a dozen of his friends screw my brains out. When we woke up late that morning, Mike, incredibly, was ready for more. I was too exhausted to do anything but lie there as he spent nearly an hour getting off a fifth time. As we lay there in each other's arms, the front door opened—my son was home! Mike made a beeline for his room, and I rushed into the bathroom and ran the shower. My son didn't notice anything, but that was the last time Mike and I had alone. As they left the next day, Mike slipped a piece of paper into my hand and gave me a wink. It was a number of a friend of his who would contact him when I wanted to see him again. My husband came home that night and we had the best sex ever—my night with Mike had done great things for our sex life. Of course, I didn't tell my husband.

I tried to resist calling Mike, but the next time my husband went out of town on business, I lasted about two hours before I was on the phone dialing Mike's friend. But that's another story.

Mike has moved out of the dorm and now has an apartment of his own. Though he has lots of girlfriends, he usually finds time for a date with me when my husband's out of town.

Mike has introduced me to a couple of his friends who join in from time to time, and I've found that having two or three guys at a time is a lot more fun than just fantasizing about it! Best of all, my husband's and my sex life is better than ever. If only he knew!

Mr. Fix-It

I am a truck driver and I often spend many lonely hours crossing some empty desert or another. But every once in a while I get an eyeful of some babe sunning herself as she passes me in her car—or, even better, a girl giving head to a guy as he drives down the road. Things like that really wake me up!

But the experience I would like to relate went beyond mere looking.

A few weeks ago I was hauling a load of cut lumber from Vancouver to Los Angeles. I was cruising through the barren San Joaquin Valley of California when I noticed a bright-red Triumph coming up behind me. I could see the driver in my mirror, a cute young thing with long blonde hair. As the car pulled even with me, the girl flashed a smile as she looked up at me through her open sunroof. She was driving in my favorite position—left foot on the seat with the knee against the door, dress pulled up almost to her crotch, with her long, tan legs and bare feet soaking up the rays and with her right hand at the bottom of the steering wheel. Her left arm was resting on the windowsill of her door. She wasn't going much faster than I was, so I gave my rig a kick and was soon pacing her, getting a good look and hoping she'd show me more.

Some girls, once they know what you are up to, will take off and leave you in the dust. Not this one. She just kept even with me, flashing that sexy smile. Naturally, I smiled back at her, glancing ahead every few seconds to make sure I wasn't about to run into anyone. Fortunately, the traffic on 1-5 was pretty light, but every once in a while she would have to speed up and pull in ahead of me to let faster traffic pass. But she always came back, each time showing a little more leg and pulling her left foot closer to her crotch.

Soon her foot was resting on the dashboard between the steering wheel and the windshield post. Then she really got daring and stuck her left foot out the window, resting her ankle on the side-view mirror. This allowed the wind to blow into her car and her dress flipped up around her navel, exposing her skimpy panties to my view! I gave her a shocked, horny look and she gave me that hot smile and threw her head back with a laugh, her blonde hair cascading over the headrest behind her. Then she ran her tongue along her teeth. She made no move to smooth her dress down! I gave her a big blast on my air horn to show my approval.

Another fast-moving truck was closing in behind her, so she pulled her foot back into the car and sped up to pull in front of my truck. As the truck passed, I gave the driver a bored-looking wave, hoping he was in too much of a hurry to notice my "lover" in the red Triumph. He was—and he didn't. As he passed the car, the woman tossed something out through her sunroof and it snagged on my right-hand windshield wiper. I flinched (I once had an owl slam through the windshield, so I am a bit jumpy about things coming at the glass) before I realized it was her panties! I couldn't believe it!!

A long line of cars passed us, following in the slipstream of the faster truck, so it was some time before my friend could move her car back over and get next to me. She had put her foot back on the mirror and her legs were spread as far as they could possibly be in the car. I got my first look at her beautiful pussy, its lips pouting out invitingly. At this point the girl began to play it cool, ignoring my presence and not looking up at me. Steering her Triumph with her right hand, she began to stroke her pussy lips with the other. Soon her hand was going a mile a minute, pulling on her clit and shoving two fingers into her pink cunt. Her left thigh began to quiver and she was chewing on her lower lip. Her sheer white dress became soaked with perspiration and I could see that she was braless. She began to hump her hand and I began to have doubts as to whether either of us was in control of his or her vehicle at that point!

She came (pun intended) back down to earth and slowed her fingers to a gentle stroking motion. She then pulled her foot back into the car and pressed her heel against her wet cunt and licked her fingers clean. Then she looked up at me with that wide smile, waved and sped off.

I was just catching my breath when I saw the Triumph swerve to the shoulder about a mile ahead of me. The right front tire had blown out, but she was able to keep the car under control and stop it safely. Being the gentleman that I am, I pulled onto the shoulder and parked behind her car to help her change the tire. She sat there, beet red in her embarrassment (I'd caught her with her pants down, as it were), but I complimented her on her performance and, as I changed the tire, she relaxed. She got out of the car and stood next to me as I worked, making small talk with me.

After I had put her spare on and jacked the car down to tighten the lug nuts, she sat on the fender, giving me another beaver shot as we talked. Her pussy was dripping wet again and only inches from my face. She smelled delicious. I cracked some dumb joke and she laughed, putting one foot on my shoulder as I tightened the last nut. Unable to resist the temptation, I pulled my gloves off and slid my hands up her legs and into the wettest pussy I have ever felt!

She immediately stopped laughing and began to moan, leaning back against the windshield post to give me complete access to her cunt. I leaned forward, pulling her to the edge of the fender, and buried my hot tongue in her slit. She tasted better than she smelled! I suddenly realized we were in full view of passing traffic and I pulled back. Fortunately, it had gotten pretty dark and no one seemed to have noticed us! She began to laugh again and got a full-blown case of the giggles. She laughed so hard that she said she had to pee. Since there were no rest rooms around for miles, I told her to go squat beside my cab where nobody could see her and to let it go, which she did.

I put the flat tire and tools in her trunk, closed the lid and walked up to her. It had apparently taken a while for her to get over her giggle-fit, because she was still squatting on the ground. "Gee," I said, "as long as you are down there, it's time to pay your bill for having your tire changed." I expected her to laugh it off, but she looked up at me with very serious eyes. I didn't blink but looked expectantly into her eyes, holding her gaze. She didn't look away but reached for my belt and said yes.

This was an immediate turn-on for me, as I have always fantasized about finding a beautiful woman who would do almost anything. I was hard already, but the way she'd said yes and the look of animal lust in her eyes almost made me come right then. I decided to play her, to see how far I could take her.

While she undid my belt, I reached down and pulled her dress off over her head and dropped it to the ground. It landed in a puddle of oil below her pussy, but she made no move to pull it out. My pants dropped to my ankles and I pushed down my shorts. She began to kiss the tip of my cock. She stroked my shaft with one hand and held on to my hip with the other, licking a drop of pre-come and trying to force her tongue into my pee-hole. She then began to lick my balls.

It had been a hot day and I could smell the sweat wafting from my crotch and I was suddenly self-conscious. But then she said, "I love the smell and taste of a man's sweat!" and began to lick under my balls and my self-consciousness went out the door. Between slurps, she told me how she had always wanted to "get down and dirty" but her husband was a wimpy "neatnik" who wouldn't let her touch him unless he was freshly showered. She wanted to revel in the taste of a "real man"—taste everything he had to offer, clean every inch of his body with her tongue. Still looking into my eyes, she said, "I'd do absolutely anything for a man who knows what he wants and is not afraid to take it!" Then she slid her mouth over my cock.

I couldn't believe what was happening! A man would have to be dead to not hear the invitation in her words and see the pleading in her eyes! I looked around to make sure we could not be seen, and, since we were completely shielded from passing cars by my truck, I went for broke. I slipped my meat into her mouth and she did not pull away. She shifted her body from the squatting position to her knees, both to steady herself against my thrusts and so she could lift her chin a little and give me access to her throat.

I moved my cock as hard and as fast as I could, sliding it easily down her throat and burying her pert nose in my pubic hair. My balls were heavy with come and made slapping noises each time they hit her chin, which was wet with saliva. I pulled out every five or six strokes so she could breathe. She loved it! So did I—and I soon let loose the largest load I think I ever have, filling her hot mouth. I held her head with my dick in her mouth until I had stopped shaking and the last few squirts had rinsed out her tonsils. She looked up at me with wild eyes, and I saw a stream of come leaking out from around my dick.

"Why don't you swallow that?" I whispered to my beautiful cocksucker. "You've never drunk a man's come, have you?" She shook her head. Again she looked at me with those blazing eyes and then gulped down my cream. It was difficult with my soft cock in the way, but after three gulps she managed to swallow it all (that's a really neat feeling, by the way).

"Did you enjoy that?" I asked. She nodded, her arms wrapped around my waist to steady herself. "Better than your husband?" Again she nodded, this time with a muffled groan. "Would you like to do it again?" Another nod and groan, and she made no attempt to pull away.

"Mmmm," she said. "I've always wanted to taste everything a man had to give, and I love it!" She put her fingers to her chin to wipe the last of the spilled jism into her mouth, but I asked her not to, to leave it there. By then I was hard again and began to slowly stroke my meat. She threw herself on my penis and began to fondle and lick it, and soon had it buried deep in her throat again. She was voracious! I surrendered myself to her hungry mouth and just stood there as she worked it in and out, up and down, making mewling noises deep in her throat until I exploded again. Again a few drops remained on her chin.

"Now please leave it there until you get to wherever you're going," I told her. She said I could count on it, and I helped her to her feet. I picked up her wet dress and walked her to her car. A truck went by and, as soon as we had a clear shot, I walked around to the driver's door of her car and opened it for her so she could slide her naked ass behind the wheel. I tossed her dress into the backseat and bent to give her a good-bye kiss, realizing it was the first time we had kissed. I tweaked her left nipple and took one last finger-dive into his pent-up semen rush to freedom and squirt out, splattering wherever it pleases.

Lisa explained to Mary that she was aware of all this, since she and I frequently rent sex videos. In fact, I was kind of amazed when Lisa candidly explained to Mary that scenes in videos—like that in *The Brat*, starring Jamie Summers—where there is lots of erotic talk between the actors and actresses, really turns us on. And (I was surprised she volunteered this) Lisa said she really enjoyed watching the semen squirt as the actors climaxed outside the actresses. To her, somehow the amount of semen ejaculated was a measure of the actor's manliness and the sexual power of the actress.

By this time, Lisa's nipples were beginning to harden and poke against the thin material of her top (I think Mary was aware of this). Anyway, after complimenting her on her beautiful body, Mary asked if she would mind taking off her top so Mary could examine her breasts. But first, Mary told Lisa, she wanted her to just stand there with her sheer top on so Mary could observe her partially covered breasts. The top was so thin that Lisa's full, medium-size breasts were visible to Mary, who commented that it looked like Lisa had nice, pointy, high-centered nipples with medium areolae. Lisa knew that it was important to impress Mary, so she offered to remove her top to provide a better look. Mary was very impressed and asked Lisa to touch her nipples so she could see them hard and erect. They were beautiful—pink, about a half inch long and a quarter inch in diameter—just like little penises crying out for stimulation.

Mary candidly asked Lisa if she realized what a delectable target her breasts would make for a swollen penis. Lisa smiled and admitted that my penis had splattered its three teaspoons of semen across her breasts many times. Mary smiled back and emphasized that the videos they were shooting called for copious male explosions on the actresses and that audiences very much enjoy watching wet climax shots. (I knew Lisa concurred one hundred percent!) Mary then told us that sex films had come a long way. Dialogue had become more important because it, too, stimulates the viewer. As a result, she explained, "There is much more erotic talk leading up to the wet climax shots. We want to tease the viewer to the max but also make him or her aware of the fact that the teasing always leads up to a wild, wet climax." Mary pointed out that, since the advent of "safe sex," masturbation has become well accepted, and that their aim was to help the viewer enjoy the masturbatory experience "just as he or she enjoys a fine meal."

Well, Lisa and I agreed. Obviously very impressed with Lisa, Mary said she needed a quick peek at Lisa's rear end and genitals. Lisa pulled her jeans down and stood there in her thin, almost transparent, panties. Mary admired the contour of Lisa's tight little butt, but when Lisa turned around, Mary's eyes lit up. Lisa's skimpy panties were very wet! She was obviously quite excited—and she was a little embarrassed, too, that Mary was seeing her in this state. Mary just stood there wordlessly, her eyes virtually devouring my sexy Lisa.

Lisa stood there and let Mary stare. Her breasts and pink nipples were gorgeous and her swollen genitals were flowering open against her almost transparent panties. It looked like Lisa's pussy was hairless, just like a little girl's—except Lisa is twenty-two years old. Most of the actresses these days like to keep their vaginal lips bare for the camera and obviously Mary wouldn't have to tell Lisa that. Mary smiled coyly as she examined Lisa's spreading pussy-petals through her panties. Mary must have sensed that I was getting awfully hot from watching all this and she told me to take off my slacks so she could examine my lower body. I was rock-hard now and my pre-come had been oozing steadily into my underwear as I watched Mary examine Lisa. By the time I pulled my slacks off and stood at attention for Mary, my penis was jutting out like a flagpole.

This was becoming an increasingly sexy situation and, not having ejaculated in four days, I was really looking forward to making Lisa a lot wetter and me several ounces lighter. I knew Mary would probably want to watch me squirt, because sex-video audiences like to see male actors make the actresses really wet, and Mary said she wanted to use men who discharge lots of semen. Well, I hadn't ejaculated yet, but the pre-come was really oozing from the little slit in my penis and dribbling down onto the rug. I think Mary thought I was about to pop, because she half smiled and quickly handed me a couple of tissues. I told her that I was leaking pre-come only because I was coveting Lisa's now totally naked, beautiful body, which was really turning me on. Mary asked Lisa to ever so gently insert her fingers in her vagina to make her sex lips flower open even wider. Mary (and I) could see plainly that Lisa was getting excited, and Lisa couldn't resist the temptation to gently rub the little pink helmet now protruding from the top of her inviting slit.

Mary said that this "interview" would be similar to the movies she would ask us to appear in, so she asked if we would mind if she watched as I penetrated Lisa. Her only request was that I shouldn't come inside Lisa, because she wanted to observe the ejaculation. I knew how important this was. As I've said, Lisa and I especially like the wet climax shots in sex videos and there is nothing worse than waiting in anticipation for the explosion, only to see a couple of weak dribbles. Lisa and I particularly like to watch Peter North–type explosions on actresses, and we knew we could show Mary just that.

Well, Lisa was really excited now. Her open labia were very swollen and hanging outside her equally inflamed inner lips. Of course, as I looked at this beautiful nymph, my penis just got harder (if that was possible) and continued to drip a thin, clear drool of pre-come onto the rug. (Gosh! What if pre-come stains rugs?) Mary was exciting us more with the suggestive comments she was making. She smiled and asked me to stand real still. Then she got down on her hands and knees and cupped my testicles in her palm. She squeezed ever so gently and commented that they seemed full enough of semen to be crying out for ejaculation.

Mary asked Lisa to bend over and then gestured for me to slide into Lisa's cunt from behind. Boy, I was looking forward to that feeling of being inside her. My penis brushed against her thighs, leaving thin trails of crystal clear pre-come fluid. Lisa giggled. In the coolness of the room, the pre-come trails were cooling quickly and kind of tickled her. As I stood close, I reached around to her beautiful breasts and massaged her pretty pink nipples between my thumbs and forefingers. It was so exciting that I felt a tremendous urge to ejaculate right there on the outside of Lisa's cunt lips. I quickly grabbed my penis and squeezed hard at the base to stop it from spurting until I was really ready. Thank goodness it worked! Oh, sure, I was still leaking pre-come, but at least my semen hadn't spilled prematurely.

As I penetrated Lisa I felt the walls of her love-tube tighten around my penis as if daring me to shoot off inside her. Lisa was on the pill, so a series of semen bursts inside her would give her only pleasure. Even so, I knew Mary wanted to watch the ejaculation just as Lisa and I do when we rent videos. Besides, Mary wanted to be sure that I performed the Peter North–type explosion that Lisa and I had talked about. When Lisa rolled over on her back and I stood up, Mary gestured for me to kneel over Lisa. As I did, Mary grabbed the head of my penis and played with the little slit, spreading pre-come all over the purple red knob. Mary smiled down at Lisa's beautiful body. Lisa's pink nipples pointed straight up from the strawberry areolae of her firm, perky breasts. Her hairless slit was by now very inflamed, of course. Mary smiled and remarked that so far we'd shown that we had the sexual capacity to fit right in with her other actors and actresses. She mentioned that occasionally Carina Collins, Candi Evens and Peter North appeared in her videos and she asked if we'd like to work with them. Lisa and I said we'd love to.

Mary grabbed my penis again and began slowly masturbating me as she reached over with her other hand to Lisa's genitals and began manipulating her clit. Lisa and I were so hot we couldn't stand it, so Mary suggested I kneel over Lisa—like I was getting ready to penetrate her in the missionary position—and just let Mary stroke my penis to climax. I remarked that I would probably spray all over Lisa's breasts and tummy. Mary grinned and said she hoped it would be as good as we told her it would be. Anyway, Mary kept stroking until I announced I wasn't able to hold back anymore. She then quickly grabbed Lisa's panties and placed them on Lisa's tummy to give me a "target." She commanded, "Fire when ready!"

I could feel the semen straining to erupt. I heard Lisa yell, "Oh, here it comes, Mary!" as the first squirt shot onto the panties. The next squirt had more pressure and hit Lisa's breasts. Then ribbon after ribbon of thick, pearly white semen sprayed all over Lisa. Mary just sat there in disbelief, watching. "Oh, my!" she finally said. The milky white sperm drops made Lisa's pretty pink nipples shine wetly. Mary touched the creamy drops with her fingers and was pleasantly surprised at how hot they were. There were numerous little puddles on Lisa's tummy and, of course, the panties were drenched. Lisa's cunt lips were still quivering from Mary's masturbatory ministrations on her clit.

Mary then said, "Let's see how you get off, Lisa!" and

started stroking Lisa faster and faster. Lisa's hips began bucking as she pumped against Mary's finger, her face contorted with pleasure. Beads of sweat began breaking out all over Lisa's torso, mixing with my milky sperm. Soon she lifted her body off the floor entirely and came.

Mary seemed very impressed and asked if we'd like to work with her video performers. We were overjoyed. "The sooner the better!" we said.

The Cockteaser and the Screaming Prick

I was eighteen and a senior in high school. It was back when all the girls wore super-short miniskirts up to their asses that drove all the guys wild, including me. There was this one girl in my class my age, Sandy, who had a fantastic body and sure knew how to strut her stuff. She was tall with long blonde hair, big firm tits and a tight little ass that was always visible when she bent over even slightly in her micro-mini-skirt. The problem was that she was one of those gold-digger types who only went out with guys who had new cars and plenty of cash to spend on her. She was a tease, strutting her stuff all around, because you knew you couldn't have a taste of that luscious body unless you had some big bucks.

The guys loved to watch her go by, but she pissed me off. One day she sat across from me in study hall. When she got up to go to the library, she swung those sleek long legs around from under her desk and gave more than a flash of the hot pink panties she was wearing. That got me really hot and bothered, but it also got me angry because she acted like she was too good to even talk to me.

One day I had just about had enough of her teasing. It was between classes and she was standing in the hall, flirting with a guy whose father owned a local construction business. She was leaning against the stairwell railing with that great ass of hers peeking out from underneath her miniskirt. The guy she was talking to left and she just stayed there looking down into the stairwell, knowing very well that her ass was drawing attention. Three of my friends were with me and they groaned aloud at the sight of her lacy white panties underneath her sheer panty hose. But I couldn't stand it anymore. As we walked by I reached out and got a firm grip on one of her ass-cheeks, gave a little squeeze and said to her, "Um, just the way I like 'em, nice and firm." She spun around instantly in a fury and said, "You son of a bitch!" I quickly replied, "You fucking tease! Quit asking for it if you don't want any!" My friends were standing by in shock, with their mouths just hanging open. I'll never forget her comeback in a million years. Without batting an eye she looked straight at me and said, "I want it bad, you just don't have enough flesh to satisfy my appetite." Howls of laughter went up from my friends as she turned victoriously and walked away. I was momentarily stunned. She won the battle, but I knew I would get her back.

From that day on it was never the same. Every time I saw her, we would jab each other with the crudest sexual insults we could think of, drawing raised eyebrows and jeers from both her friends and mine. One day we passed in the hall and I said, "Hi, cunt." She replied, "Hello, prick," and that was it. On another occasion she spouted some insult and I said, "Eat me." She turned and looked right at me and said in front of about ten witnesses, "Listen, I could suck you so hard it would make your mouth go dry." Everyone shrieked with laughter, and I was again left speechless.

This little contest went on for several weeks. Sometimes

I would be the one embarrassed and sometimes she would be. But I could tell from her reactions that she was enjoying it as much as I was—and our friends loved it.

Then came the day I will never forget. There was a Halloween carnival and dance being held in one of the school's cafeterias. Some of the students had dates, but most of us were just looking for a little excitement. I was there with two of my best friends. We clowned around at the carnival and had a pretty good time. When the dance began, we each danced with several different girls. They had a live rock band, the music was really loud and soon everyone was working themselves into a frenzy. That's about the time I spotted Sandy and her equally snooty friend Rhonda sitting near the back of the room, acting as if no guy there was good enough for them. Sandy was dressed true to form. She wore a tight pink blouse that buttoned up the front and really showed off those magnificent tits of hers. As I looked closer I could see a little lacy bra beneath the almost transparent material. She had on a super-short black miniskirt that revealed every inch of her long satiny legs, which she had crossed over her tight little pussy. She was definitely a turn-on, but I ignored her as best I could and danced with a couple other girls who were close friends of mine. Still, just knowing she was sitting there aggravated the hell out of me.

Then the band announced that they were going to play a couple of slow songs and the lights went dim. The band started playing softly. I was looking around for a partner and spotted Sandy still sitting in the same chair. I thought to myself, "Oh, what the hell, give it a try." I walked over to her and was just about to ask her to dance when she turned her head, glared at me and snapped, "What the hell do you want?" Quick with a reply, I bent over and whispered in her ear, "I want to come inside of you." She was stunned. Without asking, I took her by the arm and led her out to the dance floor. I looked into her eyes. She wasn't embarrassed—she was melting with desire. I placed my hands on her waist and pulled her to me. She wrapped her arms around my neck as if we were old lovers and started swaying to the music. I could feel her firm breasts heaving against my chest. I had an instant hard-on. She pressed against me so forcefully that I knew she could feel every throbbing inch of me.

As the music went on she really started getting into it. She eventually worked my right leg in between her legs and started a slight up-and-down humping motion on my upper thigh. Her tiny skirt rode up slightly and I could feel her wet warmth on my leg as she ground her panty-hose-covered pussy into me. I reached underneath her skirt and grabbed her ass with both hands. She moaned softly and rested her face on my shoulder. There were other couples all around us, but no one noticed our activity because the room was so dark and crowded. When I began to caress her tight ass with my fingers I realized that I could feel nothing but a thin layer of nylon. She was not wearing any panties—only panty hose that were sheer to the waist! Then, just when I was about to slide my fingers down her ass into her wetness, the lights came on and the song ended. Suddenly she jerked her head up, pushed me roughly away and said, "You bastard!" I was taken entirely by surprise and just stood there and watched her walk back to her seat where her friend Rhonda was still sitting. A friend of mine came to me and said, "What's wrong, Romeo? Trying to get in her pants again?" But I was too bothered to give him a reply. I was hot and could feel my juices dribbling from my massive tool. And I was pissed off too! How could she be such a teasing little bitch?

I walked off the dance floor and looked over at her again. She was sitting there with her legs tightly crossed and her arms folded smugly across her chest, acting as if she were the princess of the ball. But I knew that her hot pussy had been gushing just a minute ago. What a bitch! If she had thought that I had had a new car sitting out in the parking lot, she would have eagerly hopped into my backseat and fucked my balls off.

I was just about ready to ignore her again when I saw her lean over to her friend and whisper something. Then she got up and went through a door which led into the adjoining kitchen area. Since this area was restricted, I wanted to know what she was up to. So I waited a few seconds and then followed her. The kitchen was completely dark but, after my eyes adjusted, I saw that she had gone outside through an exit that led to the truck loading dock. I quietly stepped out into the darkness. The area was fenced off from the school yard, surrounded by tall evergreen trees. I couldn't figure out where Sandy had gone. Then I heard a familiar low moan from the dark corner of the loading dock near a small stack of packing crates. I squinted my eyes and made out Sandy's form, facing away from me. She was moaning because she had her skirt pulled up and seemed to be furiously frigging her hot pussy with her right hand. What a magnificent performance she was putting on, and all for me!

My cock was throbbing and so hard that I couldn't just stand there anymore. As I came up slowly behind her, she became aware of my presence, quickly smoothed down her skirt and stood up. I walked right up behind her, pressed my body close to hers and whispered in her ear, "Need some help?" She silently responded by easing her body back into mine. She wanted me badly! She started to turn to face me, but I wrapped my arms around her waist and pulled her ass to my crotch. She began to rotate her hips and I slowly massaged my way up her belly until I had both of her beautiful tits cupped in my palms. She leaned her head back on my shoulder and moaned. I could feel her stiff nipples through her thin pink blouse and her lacy bra. I leaned over and bit her gently on her neck. She let out a little squeal and pressed back into me more forcefully. Then she took my hand from her breast and placed it on her upper thigh. I began to massage her leg just below the hem of her skirt. I could feel the wetness that was seeping down from her passion pit and I could faintly smell its gentle scent in the fresh autumn air. I worked slowly upward until I had her hot pussy quivering under my fingers. The front of her panty hose was so soaked with her juices that my fingers were wet. She was almost screaming now. There was no stopping us.

As I continued to finger her nylon-covered cunt, I used my other hand to undo my pants and drop my shorts. I pulled up the back of her skirt and my cock sprang up between her legs and snuggled up into her hot wet junction. She reached down in front of her and grasped my cock, sticking out from between her legs. I began to piston back and forth as she held it tightly against her sopping mop. She was really getting hot. She would lean forward, roll her head around, then throw her long blonde hair back over her shoulder and lean back into me again, moaning louder with each of my strokes.

Finally she could stand it no longer. She stuck her thumbs inside the waistband of her panty hose and jerked her nylons down around her knees. She leaned over the stack of crates with her ass sticking up provocatively, looked back at me and said in a low lusty voice, "Do it!" I placed my cock between her now naked thighs and felt the warmth of her hot flesh. I figured that she wanted my steel shaft jammed up into her hot little hole, so I decided to do a little teasing of my own. Besides, I knew I wouldn't last long if I plunged right into her and I wanted this ecstasy to last just a little longer. I reached around in front of her and pulled my cock up between her cunt lips and slowly began to rub the length of my shaft against her protruding clit. She started bucking wildly and said, "No, I need you to put it in me!" But I just kept right on sliding gently back and forth in between the folds of her hot muff. She arched her back and leaned her chest against the crate she was using for support. She groaned in frustration a couple of times and tried to work the knob of my prick into her dripping tunnel, but I wouldn't let her have it. She was going to have to beg for it!

Finally she looked back over her shoulder with a fire in her eyes and said, "Fuck me, you bastard!" That was good enough. I eased back and placed the tip of my huge dong at the entrance to her quivering hole. Then I thrust forward and my whole length sank into her depths in one mighty stroke. She screamed out loud. It was tight, but she was so lubricated that I went in all the way. My size was more than she expected, but as I began my thrusts, she matched me stroke for stroke. I reached forward and got my hands on both her tits inside her blouse as I continued to pound away at her box. Her breathing got very rapid and shallow in between moans. Soon my balls were boiling with liquid and I knew that I would last only a few more strokes. I pounded hard. Then she really got wild. She started screaming, "Oh, shit, oh shit, oh fuck, oohh fuck, ooohhh . . ." That did it! In the middle of her intense orgasm I blasted the biggest load of jism of my entire life! Wad after wad pumped out into her steamy depths as she continued to moan softly.

My prick began to go soft, but I continued to stroke slowly in and out of her cunt until at last my limp noodle slipped out of her. While we were both trying to catch our breaths, our juices were running down the inside of her thighs. We stayed there in that position for several minutes, hearing nothing but the pounding of our hearts. Finally I put myself back in my pants and she pulled her soaking wet panty hose back into place. She turned around to face me for the first time in the encounter. She planted a passionate wet kiss on me, snaking her tongue in between my lips. Then she just looked at me for a moment with those big blue eyes. We went back to the dance but she went her way and I went mine. We became good friends that year but never again repeated our sexual encounter. Today she is married to a well-to-do broker. Wouldn't you know it! All in all, Sandy has to rank as one of the best lays of my life. Although I now rarely see her, I'm told she's reverted to her cockteasing ways—who knows, I might get lucky again.

Hot Rods and Rubber Dolls

Saturday was a typical northern California spring day. I decided to enjoy the sun and generate some sweat at the same time by riding my mountain bike. After I got to my favorite riding area, I took off at a fast clip down a winding trail. As I climbed a small knoll, something off to the right caught my eye. I stopped short, only to glimpse what appeared to be a naked woman near the top of the hill. My curiosity, as well as my lecherous mind, urged me to head in that direction. I was trying to be quiet, hoping that my eyes had not deceived me. I didn't want to blow a chance at spying on some babe in the buff.

In fact, I decided to walk the rest of the way. I laid down my bike and crept slowly, silently, toward the summit. When I reached the top of the hill, what I saw caught me off guard. About fifteen yards below me was a very attractive redhead. My first impression had been correct—she was indeed naked. But what really made my eyeballs pop out of their sockets was that she was fucking one of those blowup sex dolls! Here was this voluptuous woman balling a hunk of rubber!

I couldn't help but laugh out loud at the sight. I thought she heard me for a moment when she stopped fucking briefly and looked up the hill. I just lay low for a couple minutes before taking another look. I didn't get up and go over to her because I was deeply curious about what kind of crazy sex she was going to have with her rubber Romeo.

When I glanced her way again, I saw that she had gone back to French-kissing her "lover." Carefully she ran her tongue around the doll's puckered lips while lustfully moaning out loud. From my vantage point I could see that this woman was endowed with a hefty set of knockers. Even from fifteen yards away, each of her nipples appeared to be the size of my thumb! Her pussy had been cleanly shaved and I could clearly see the large outer lips of her cunt. She positioned the doll on top of her and placed its erect penis between her legs. I remember thinking that she may have filled it with water instead of air, because the doll appeared to be quite heavy. What a bizarre scene! After a few minutes of masturbating her pussy with the doll's cock, she ran its dick slowly up along her body, stopping at her breasts. She rubbed its erection between them, pushing them together and lifting her head to watch the action. Eventually she moved the imitation cock up so she could take it into her mouth, and she gave the thing one of the wildest blowjobs I've ever witnessed.

By this time, my own dick was throbbing with excitement. I pulled down my shorts, grabbed it with both hands and, in a frenzy, started to jerk off. My balls were swollen with come that was just pulsing to shoot out, and I wasn't about to stop stroking. I turned my attention back to the woman just as she rolled over on top of her blowup doll. I could even hear what she was saying. Was it ever dirty! With the plastic man's cock in one hand and his face in the other, she was calling him a "weak bastard" and rasping, "I'm going to fuck you so hard your balls will turn black and blue." Picture this very feminine-looking woman fucking a sex doll, mouthing these filthy words. Then she did exactly as she said she'd do to her inflated sex toy. Her humping was so fast and furious I thought for sure her buddy was about to burst. All I could feel was envy for a piece of rubber—that and the buildup in my groin. I couldn't hold back any longer and my come surged through my dick, spurting all over my bare belly and chest. I went rigid as my orgasm jolted my entire nervous system. After that, my eyes glazed over and I passed out.

I thought I was fantasizing again when I felt a warm, moist sensation on my lower abdomen. I opened my eyes enough to see the very same woman running her talented tongue across my belly toward my dick. Was I dreaming? I leaned forward and saw that it was, indeed, the redhead. She asked if she had been the one who'd caused all the mess, referring to the come that was splattered all over my belly. Not quite believing what was happening, I just shook my head yes. With her hungry mouth sucking on my limp cock, she aroused an animal lust in me like I've never felt before. I lay back, closed my eyes and smiled. I'm not made of rubber . . .

Working Late

Karen and I had been working in the same office for over a year before we met at lunch one day and discovered that we had much in common. It didn't take long before we were meeting for most of our lunchtimes. Karen stands about five feet two inches tall, has long blonde hair that reaches down to the small of her back, soft blue eyes and full, pouting lips—a real doll.

During the summer, she often wore tight-fitting miniskirts and T-shirts that looked like they were spray-painted on her body. Several times I'd met her dashing across the parking lot to get out of a sudden, soaking summer rain. The damp chill would cause her nipples to stand erect in her skimpy bra and her shirt to cling to her ample breasts, which rose enticingly with her every breath. Hiding my erections during these encounters was often a problem.

Our relationship began in earnest one night when I was at my desk, long after regular working hours. Growing drowsy, I got up and took a walk around the hallways to see who else was burning the late-night oil. As I was passing the elevator, the doors opened and Karen emerged.

Karen was wearing a one-piece cotton sundress that clung

to her luscious body suggestively and was short enough to provide spicy glimpses of milady's thighs. Actually, she might almost as well have been wearing Saran Wrap, for her dress was soaked and virtually transparent. Her nipples appeared as hard points on her beautiful breasts, and the lace fringes of her underwear were visible, perfectly framing her luscious cunt lips.

"Just when I found that my car wouldn't start, the rain came crashing down," she said. My raging hard-on and I both thanked the powers-that-be. "Do you think you could give me a jump start?" she asked.

"Of course," I stammered. "I'll be done in just a bit." I tore my gaze from her fetching breasts, which seemed to be crying out to me to be kissed and squeezed. My heartbeat was racing as I returned to my desk and resumed working. Karen followed. She sat on the edge of my desk, almost as if it was her intention to drive me wild. Maybe she was horny, maybe she had tied on a few, lowering her inhibitions, or maybe she was a lot more courageous than I dared to hope. After a few minutes, she lay back languidly and pulled her dress farther up her thighs.

As I sat in awe and watched her breathe, she spoke. "Have you ever thought of all the different places in this building that would be great for having sex?" she asked. I couldn't believe what I'd just heard! I thought I would lose my load right then and there. "How about it?" she proposed. "It's late and the place is deserted. And you did offer to help me."

That was all the urging I needed. Without a word, I shut off my desk lamp and stood up. I laid my hands on her thighs as I positioned myself in between them. I raised her dress and moved my hands up her smooth thighs to her lace-covered snatch. Her rain-dampened panties slid over my fingers and, with my thumbs, I began lightly stroking her crack. I could feel the heat of her body as I reached around her firm ass and pulled her closer. She reached up, pulled my head close and kissed me as I'd never been kissed before. She then unzipped my pants. Her small hands trembled as she wrapped them around my straining member and pulled it forth. I pulled her toward me across the smooth desktop and got into position to start fucking.

"Whoa! Hold on!" she said. She got off the desk and deftly pulled her dress over her head, letting it fall to the floor. That done, she knelt and helped me remove my pants and undershorts. Seeing my eight-incher standing tall, she sucked it between her full lips and flicked her tongue back and forth across its swollen tip. I felt her hot breath at the base of my shaft as she sucked and kissed every inch. My first load had almost arrived when she suddenly stood up and walked out into the hallway.

"That was just to make sure you're really ready!" she said as she left the office. I promptly followed. She went to the drinking fountain and splashed water on her breasts before turning to face me. I could see a passionate desire in her eyes. Her breath was shallow and labored. The cool water of the fountain had brought her nipples to full attention, and I began to kiss them. She sighed deeply with my every kiss and caress. I reached behind her to grasp her firm ass and to remove the last of her garments. She moaned and purred as I pushed her panties slowly down her thighs, and she stepped out of them. Placing my hands on her ass again, I pulled her against my rigid cock. She began massaging it. Only an enormous exercise of willpower kept me from going over the edge.

But then, with no warning, she tore herself free. She ran away from me and vanished around a bend in the corridor. I hurried after her, eager to find her and quench the flames of my desire in her moist, pink love sluice.

Standing out before me like a divining rod, my cock seemed

to direct me to her. She was waiting in the storeroom. The door closed quietly behind me as I entered the darkened room. Without warning, her lips were on mine, burning with lust and desire. I hugged her hot body to mine and she wrapped her legs around my waist. My throbbing prick effortlessly penetrated her warm, moist cunt. Immediately I felt that amazing, massaging grip that every horny woman possesses in her vagina.

Holding her ass, I directed her up and down on my straining tool. Whenever her legs tightened about me, the muscles in her snatch gripped the shaft of my cock tighter. I could feel the suction growing as our thrusts increased in strength and tempo. I'd never felt a pussy so fantastically tight before! Our rocking motion pulled at the foundations of my being as the fantastic Karen screwed me for all I was worth. The delicious pleasure mounted as her sex juices began to run down my legs.

Karen arrived at her first climax with a rush. She arched her back, let out a deep moan, and pushed her breasts up toward my face. I continued driving wildly into her. Her wild abandon soon sent me over the top. With a low grunt as the air whooshed from my lungs. I pressed my savage member as deeply as possible into her box and shot my sperm into her voracious depths.

I slowly withdrew from her and slumped to the floor. She sat beside me and we both gasped for air, grinning like idiots.

After a few minutes, I heard an impish giggle and saw Karen get up and walk toward the door. "Why don't you just relax for a minute while I go and retrieve our clothes?" she said. When she'd left the room, I stood up and headed down the hallway to the conference room, where I collapsed into one of the chairs. I guess I must have dozed off, because the next thing I remembered was feeling the weight of Karen's body on my lap. I opened my eyes and saw her bare backside.

"We can't possibly have any more fun until I get you ready again," she said in that fetching tone of hers. Then she began slowly moving her ass back and forth across my rising dick. Her sighs filled the room as I reached around her and began massaging her firm breasts and rock-hard nipples. With one hand I began caressing her cleavage. With my other hand I reached down to her pink cleft and began massaging her hard clitoris.

As Karen's bucking and moaning increased, my dick sprang up to its full height and begged for attention. The sweat on her thighs helped her slide across my lap almost effortlessly. The friction of my prick against her beautiful ass felt delightful. Reaching down, she deftly slid my mammoth member into her well-lubricated snatch and began to ride me with zeal. Her panting grew louder and louder as she neared another climax. With one hand she was rubbing the base of my pecker and delicately massaging my nuts while her other hand was guiding my touches upon her burning flesh.

Just as Karen orgasmed we were startled to hear a key in the door and someone turning the knob. Fearing discovery, Karen—still in the midst of her climax—quickly got off of me and hid under the large conference table. When the cleaning lady entered the room, I laid my wet trousers over Karen's white dress. The cleaning lady looked at me curiously. I tried to explain that I had accidentally soaked myself in the thundershower and had come upstairs to dry off. Under the table, Karen took my stiff cock into her mouth and began to lick and suck it. I did my best to cover up my trouserless condition from the intruding woman while Karen brought me ever closer to my second orgasm with her lips and tongue. As the familiar pressure rose in my nuts, I was forced to account for my involuntary thrusting motions, lest the intruder catch on to what was happening. I explained that I was cold and shivering, and I pointedly asked her to turn out the lights when she left. But still this woman remained to chat! I couldn't have borne it if Karen were to stop—her blowjob was making my face tingle as that delicious pressure reached a crescendo in my balls. Sensing the nearness of my climax, Karen dramatically increased the tempo, all the while maintaining a perfect silence below the table.

"You don't look so good," the cleaning woman said. "Maybe you've taken a chill!"

I was about to assure her of my well-being when I ejaculated with frightening force. As gobs of my hot load filled Karen's mouth, my hands shot out across the tabletop and my eyes began tearing. As my hips pushed forward, I involuntarily caused Karen's head to bang against the table. The cleaning woman jumped back as if I had leapt at her, brandishing her vacuum hose as if to ward me off, and fled.

After she had slammed the door, I looked under the table and saw Karen sitting there with a big satisfied grin on her face. "Thanks so much!" she said. "I have meetings in here all the time, and doing this is about all that I can ever think of." As I helped her out from under the table, she gave me a long kiss. I assured her that whenever she felt this daring again, I would be more than happy to oblige her!

The Couple and the Bachelor

My wife Liz and I are both thirty years old. We are an attractive couple. Both of us are in great shape, with well-tanned bodies, and we like to remain that way. We live in a quiet subdivision and have a secluded patio in our backyard where we sunbathe nude every chance we get.

The house next to ours was recently occupied by a new neighbor, a bachelor. After about a week, Liz and I decided to extend a friendly invitation for him to come over for a get-acquainted drink. Liz said she would go over during the afternoon and introduce herself while I was at work. She said that she had very little on when she went next door to extend the invitation, which is how she usually dresses in the summer. All she wore was a tiny halter top that was just about transparent, and a pair of short shorts. The halter afforded a great view of her tits and dark-brown nipples, while the shorts left almost half her ass in plain sight. When I got home, I asked Liz how things had gone. She said that our new neighbor, Phil, would be over after dinner for drinks. She also told me that he was attractive, about forty years old and living alone. He had seemed very nice and easygoing, and he was happy that someone had come over to visit.

Phil arrived at about eight o'clock with a bottle of wine. I introduced myself. Liz was upstairs showering, so I opened the wine and poured a glass for Phil and myself. While we drank and waited for Liz, Phil told me he worked as a consultant to a large company in the area, and that he'd always wanted to move out here. Liz came down about twenty minutes later and joined us. Liz likes to dress sexy. Very much an exhibitionist, she wore a long nightgown slit up the front almost to her crotch and so low-cut on top that it revealed more than a little of her beautiful big tits. Judging from the grin on his face, Phil was pleased to see her again. When she sat on the sofa across from Phil and me, we had a great view of her long legs, which were exposed by the slit in her gown. Liz has the best body I have ever seen. She has a perfectly conditioned 35–23–37 figure and stands five feet ten inches tall in her bare feet.

We were all very relaxed and enjoying each other's company. It was turning out to be a great night. The wine was helping things along. I mentioned to Liz that I thought she was wrong about Phil being forty, and Phil said he was actually forty-two. In utter disbelief, she asked him how he kept himself so young-looking. He said he exercised a lot outdoors and loved being in the sun, which was apparent from the nice tan he had. Liz told him how much we enjoyed sunbathing in our backyard. She didn't mention that we usually do it naked, though. Phil said he preferred going to the beach to tan, adding that he wished there was one nearby. Liz told him that he was more than welcome to try out the backyard beach and join us on our patio the next afternoon. Phil thanked her and said he'd be over.

After some more talk, Liz got up to get us all another glass of wine. As she leaned over to hand Phil his glass, her tits almost fell out of her gown. He couldn't take his eyes off of her, and I couldn't blame him. As I've said, Liz enjoys being an exhibitionist as much as I enjoy being a voyeur. When she sat down on the sofa again, her gown was so far above her knees that we could see she wasn't wearing panties. Making sure we had a good view of her tits as well, she moved the material of her bodice very discreetly aside, so that both breasts were all but revealed down to the upper edges of her areolae.

When we were ready for more wine, Liz said we'd finished the bottle. Since it was still early, I volunteered to go out for more. Phil said he would take a ride with me. On the way to the liquor store, he told me how attractive Liz was and how lucky I was to have her. I remarked on how much she would appreciate hearing him say that to her directly. Phil said that, if I didn't mind, he'd express his admiration to her when we got back. I told him just to relax and tell her whatever was on his mind, because Liz and I were always very open with each other. I think my assurance helped Phil to relax a lot.

Soon we were back, sitting around talking, the two of us men watching Liz. When Phil did mention how attractive he found her, Liz smiled happily and said thank you. He surprised me then by adding that she had a body he would love to see more of. Liz was seated facing us and, as she crossed her legs, we were able to get a glance at her crotch, but only for a split second. Her top was pushed further aside, however, giving us a full view of her areolae. Liz certainly knew exactly what to do to drive us nuts. This went on for the rest of the night, till Phil said that he should be going. As we walked him to the door, Liz told him to be sure to stop by the next day to work on his tan. He said he'd be there and thanked us both for a very nice evening.

After Phil's departure, Liz and I stayed up and talked

awhile. She said again that she couldn't believe Phil was over forty and she wondered if he was as good at sex as his body led her to believe. She had always wanted to have an older man, just to see what it would be like. I said that this might be a golden opportunity for her to satisfy her curiosity. (As I've said, we are very open with each other, sexually as well as otherwise.) I also said I was sure—judging from what he'd said—that Phil would not mind putting his body at her service.

Next morning, we got up early and laid out several blankets on the patio. Then I went to the corner store for beer and put it in a cooler on the patio. A radio completed our sunbathing gear. Liz and I, not wishing to force matters, decided not to greet Phil in the nude, but rather to wait and see what happened. I wore a bikini that barely covered my cock and ass. (If I couldn't be naked, at least I'd cover as little as possible.) Liz chose to wear the skimpiest bikini that she had. Made of a satiny material, it always gets men's attention. The top consisted of a tiny string that barely covered her tits and showed most of her nipples. The bottom was a G-string that didn't cover her ass at all. The best part was that the G-string covered nothing more than the slit of her completely hairless (shaven) pussy.

Before I went outside to get things ready, while I was oiling myself up with suntan lotion, the doorbell rang. It was Phil, and he asked if he was late, seeing that I was already oiled up and in my bikini. I said no, and commented that it was already eighty degrees, but it was only ten o'clock in the morning. I noticed that Phil was checking me out. He told me that he liked the bikini I was wearing. I thanked him and thought nothing more of it. Phil then said that under his shorts and tank top, he was wearing a bikini similar to mine. I told him that I thought it would please Liz that both of us guys were wearing bikinis.

When Phil and I walked outside. Liz came over to say hello to Phil. His eyes almost bugged out when he saw her in her string bikini. She told him to take off his outer clothes and relax. As Liz walked back to the patio. Phil noticed that there was nothing covering her ass-cheeks, and he just followed her as she shook them all the way there. Liz decided that we should all have a beer, and when she bent over the cooler to get them, the view of her ass was fantastic. Phil thanked Liz for the beer and told her how well her bikini showed off her fantastic body. Liz said she was glad that he liked it—and her body as well. Phil took off his top, revealing a hairless and very muscular chest. Liz watched intently as he took off his shorts. His bikini was almost as small as mine, and he had a nice big bulge in his crotch. Liz said that he also looked good in his bikini, and that she liked what it showed off. Phil's trim, hard body was nicely tanned.

Liz said she was going to put on some oil, and she gave Phil the other bottle to use. Phil and I were mesmerized as we watched her slowly massage the oil into her skin. She started with her shoulders and then did her tits, sliding her oily hand under the string bra and getting her huge nipples hard. She worked down across her stomach toward her pussy, teasing us like mad. Liz then stood up, rested one foot on a chair and rubbed oil up the length of her leg to her crotch. She repeated this performance with her other leg. Phil and I watched as she seductively turned around and massaged oil into her buttocks and the crack of her ass. When she finished, she asked me to put oil on her back. I did so gladly, kissing her neck as well.

At this point, I wasn't the only one with a hard-on. It was obvious that Phil had one, too, as Liz noticed when he started to oil himself up. She wryly commented on how he and I seemed to be enjoying what we saw. Phil said he was enjoying it very much, at which Liz offered to oil his back for him.

When we were all oiled up, Liz suggested that we play some Frisbee before it got too hot. It was a good idea on her part because it gave Phil and me a good chance to watch her tits bouncing. We also had some great shots of her ass whenever she bent over to pick up the Frisbee. It was a miracle that her tits remained in her skimpy top.

We tossed the Frisbee around for about half an hour, then sat down for a few beers and some conversation, which eventually turned to sex. Phil said that he had never married and did not have much chance to date because of his heavy work schedule. He also said he didn't have any other friends out here and was glad to know us. Liz said that maybe she could help him out. She explained that she and I have an open marriage. Much to my surprise, she also told him that I was bisexual. (Although I am, I didn't expect her to bring it up.) Her next statement was even more surprising for she said that I could help him out too.

Phil wasn't at all upset. He simply said that he had been curious about bisexuality for some time. He also mentioned to Liz that he would give anything to have sex with an attractive girl like her, with a body like hers. Liz just smiled. It was obvious that the sunshine and beer had mellowed the three of us out, and that things were opening up. We sat around and drank several more beers, getting pretty loaded. After a while, Liz suggested that we lie back and work on our tans.

Liz was between Phil and me as we lay on our stomachs, soaking up rays. She offered to oil us up again if, when she was done, one of us would do the same for her. That was fine with Phil and me. Deciding to do me up first, Liz gave Phil a nice view as she kneeled by me, facing him. When Liz got to my crotch, she gently gave my balls a squeeze. When she was done spreading oil on me, she leaned over and gave my ear a nice wet tongue-kiss.

When she asked if Phil was ready for his oiling he was lying on his side with a huge erection visible. Seeing the bulge at his crotch, Liz quipped that it looked like he was ready. She told him not to be embarrassed, that she was happy she made him feel sexy. Phil relaxed and asked if he would get the same kind of oil rub as I'd had. She said he surely would, but she gave him a much slower massage, especially when she got to the part of his thighs closest to his crotch. I saw her rub his ass and give his balls a squeeze. Phil even let out a soft moan. At the end of her massage, she even kissed his ear as she'd kissed mine. I got a giant hard-on just from watching all this.

Liz then asked which of us was going to return the favor and oil her body. Phil looked at me questioningly. I told him to be my guest. I knew that this was what Liz wanted. With his erection still intact, Phil rubbed oil upon Liz's smooth skin from her shoulders to her toes. When he got to her string top, Liz told him to untie it. The string fell off of her, enabling us to see the sides of her tits, which were pressed against the blanket as she lay on her stomach. When Phil reached her ass, he tactfully moved on by it to her feet, but Liz said to him, "Hey, don't forget my ass, if you please." Phil replied that he wanted to leave the best part for last. He gave her feet a nice massage and started to work his hands back up her legs. Liz began to moan and squirm around as Phil's hands approached her crotch. She was also spreading her legs wider and wider apart. She told him to take all the time he needed—and, believe me, he did. Liz's legs were spread as far apart as I had ever seen them, which gave Phil a great view of her ass and pussy, neither of which was much concealed by her bikini. When he began massaging her inner thighs, he let his fingers glide across her smooth skin. Then he knelt between her legs and let his fingers slide between the cheeks of her ass. Liz was really moaning and squirming as Phil finished up with a kiss like the one she had given to each of us. Liz thanked him for an excellent job and said that, if he was willing, she would like him to repeat that later on her front side. Phil said he would love to oblige, if it was all right with me. I said that whatever Liz wanted would be fine with me. Phil thanked us both, and we lay in the sun for another hour and a half, the whole time downing beers.

Finally, Liz said that we'd better turn over so we wouldn't get sunburned on our backs. As we stood and stretched, Phil excused himself to go to the bathroom. While he was gone, Liz asked if I minded the way things were going. I said no, not at all, that I'd enjoyed just watching. She assured me that I would not be left out of the fun later that day. I said I wasn't worried about that, and she gave me a kiss and said thanks for understanding.

When Phil returned, I left for the bathroom. When I reached the door of the house, I saw Liz and Phil engaged in a deep kiss. They didn't hesitate at all—it must have been the beer, or maybe they'd kissed before. I went inside without saying anything. When I returned, they were still kissing, so I waited until they were done before I rejoined them. We sprawled on our backs, and Liz said it was her turn again to apply the oil. She started with me. I hadn't lost my erection from before—it was even larger, in fact. Starting at my shoulders, she spread oil upon my upper torso. At one point, she grabbed my nipples between her fingers and gave them a pinch. Then she put her mouth on them and sucked and gently bit them. She knew I was dying for her to do that, and she kept it up for several minutes before moving on with her hands.

Watching all this, Phil got another huge hard-on. Liz told him to be patient because he was in for the same treatment. But he began rubbing his cock through his bikini as he watched. When Liz reached my crotch and saw the bulge there, she asked Phil if he would mind if she peeled my swimsuit off of me, explaining that we normally lay out naked anyway. He said it would be fine with him. With that, Liz pulled the bikini off of me, exposing my rigid prick, which stood straight up. I have a good eight-incher with a large pink head. Liz teased a little by caressing my cock and balls, then continued the massage down my legs. When she noticed the drops of pre-come on my cockhead, she leaned down and licked them up. But then she stopped and asked Phil if he was ready.

Judging from how swelled up his cock looked in his bikini, he was beyond mere readiness. After making sure that I had a good view, Liz gave him the best massage I had ever seen. Phil was moaning louder than before. I was a little surprised—and disappointed too—that she did not take off his bikini when she got to it. When Phil looked at her questioningly, she told him that she wanted to leave the best part for last, which made him smile happily. When she did take Phil's bikini off, it seemed to take forever. I was just as anxious as Liz was to see his prick—and we were both rewarded by the sight of the largest cock either of us had ever drooled over. It had to be at least three inches longer than mine. The head resembled a dark purple plum. Liz began to rub oil over it with both of her hands, working up and down the length of the shaft and then cupping his balls. It was several minutes before she finished with a hot kiss upon the head. It was amazing that neither Phil nor I had come yet. I think that beer must inhibit sperm production somehow.

Liz asked Phil if he was ready to give her the repeat massage he had promised. Phil told her to lie on her back. Before she did so, she said she wanted to give us a better look at her titties. With that, she reached behind her back and untied her top (which she had earlier retied). Her firm round tits were revealed for our joyous inspection. Her nipples were hard, almost an inch long, and begging for attention. Phil commented that he had never seen bigger nipples and that he loved their rich brown color. Liz suggested that he shouldn't waste time talking about them.

Phil poured oil on her and began to rub it in, trying not to rush directly to her tits. Finally, though, he began to play with them. Liz begged him to pinch and pull her nipples. The more he played with them, the more she loved it, moaning louder all the time. Phil kept pleasuring her tits for at least ten minutes before massaging the rest of her. He seemed apprehensive about taking off her bikini bottom, until Liz forthrightly requested him to do so. He then untied the waist string. Liz raised her midsection a little so as to make it easier for him to remove the little triangle of fabric. When he got a full view of Liz's bald pussy, he couldn't believe his eyes. It was the first shaved cunt he'd ever seen, he said, exclaiming how beautiful it looked with all the hair removed. Liz said she was glad he liked it. I moved over for a better look and saw that her pussy was dripping with juices. Phil noticed this too. Without asking, he knelt between her legs and began to lick her entire snatch. Liz began going wild. She thrashed around and made little squeals of ecstasy as Phil pushed his tongue between her cunt lips.

I began to masturbate as I watched the show unfold in front of me. Liz must have had several orgasms during the few minutes that Phil was eating her cunt. When he stopped, she looked drained. She said it was time for her to do more than just look at the two big cocks within her reach. She suggested that, unless Phil and I objected, she wanted to give us both head at the same time. It was fine with us, we told her. So she had us stand alongside each other while she knelt in front of us. Taking hold of our pricks, she pulled us together until our pricks were touching. I looked at Phil, who said it felt good to have another cock against his. Liz rubbed them gently against each other for a while. Then she began to lick them both at the same time. I hadn't thought it possible, but Liz managed to stuff both of our dicks into her mouth at once. It wasn't easy, but she did suck on a few inches of both simultaneously and to lick the heads with her hot tongue.

Phil and I could have gone on like that for hours, but Liz finally had to stop. She got on all fours and asked Phil to fuck her doggie-style. She then asked me to eat her at the same time Phil was fucking her. I lay beneath her, my head under her pussy, and I spread her meat apart as I watched Phil's long, hard cock sliding in and out of my wife's cunt. It was a sight I had never seen from this angle before. After he had gotten his entire shaft in her, I began to lick her clit and kiss as much of her pussy as I could. The whole time I was doing this, Phil's prick was running across my tongue, and his balls, which were huge, were slapping my face. Phil and Liz soon were thrashing wildly. They began to fuck each other harder and harder. Nevertheless, Liz somehow leaned her head down and began to suck my cock. She and I had never been in a position like this before, but we were loving it—as, I am sure, Phil was too.

After about five minutes of getting head from Liz, I announced that I was ready to come. Phil said that he couldn't hold back any longer himself. At almost the same moment, we both exploded. I fired my hot come in Liz's mouth, and she greedily swallowed every drop. Phil, meanwhile, kept pumping his load deep into my wife's pussy. Still licking her there, I tasted Phil's sperm when it began to drip out. When Phil finally withdrew that huge cock of his, Liz asked me not to move because she had a treat for me. I remained under her, and she lowered her pussy until she was sitting on my face. I knew then what my treat was. Phil's come was dripping profusely from Liz's pussy and into my mouth. She normally has lots of juice for me to enjoy, but now there was so much more—and it tasted especially good—with Phil's come mixed in. I swallowed every last drop.

After I'd had my treat, Liz said we should get out of the sun. The sun and the beer were getting to me too, so I said we should move to the hammock, which is strung beneath some shade trees in the corner of our yard. Phil and Liz thought that was a great idea. We all lay down again in the hammock and fell asleep. We were out for an hour or so and woke up feeling great. We discussed what had happened and agreed it had been great. As we talked, we all got horny again. Phil and I soon had hard-ons again, and Liz began playing with her nipples and fingering her pussy.

Phil and I sat back against the ropes and stroked ourselves as we watched. When Liz was done coming, she said it was our turn to masturbate while she watched. Phil and I moved to the opposite side of the hammock so she had a good view of our hard dicks. We began to jerk off as she gently played with her tits and pussy. I had an urge to grab Phil's cock, but I wasn't sure how he would react, even though he'd said he was curious about what a bi encounter would be like. As though she were reading my mind, Liz said that maybe I could help Phil out. He looked apprehensive but said it would be all right with him, so I pulled him toward me until our chests were touching. The hammock was like a giant pocket, holding the two of us together like two peas in a pod as we gently rocked back and forth. At that point I forgot that my wife seemed to be infatuated with our new neighbor; in fact, I forgot she was even there. I was completely focused on Phil's beautiful, hairless chest. I kissed his nipples and bit them gently. I inhaled his strong, salty man-smell as I reached down and began to rub our cocks together, stroking them both at the same time. Then I reached around and cradled his buns, which were still slippery from with suntan oil. Before I even had time to think about it, Phil was kissing me, hard on the lips. His tongue found my tongue and his chest rose and fell against mine as his breathing quickened.

I was beginning to understand what my wife saw in him—
he was a great kisser. I could have kissed him the rest of the
afternoon, but there were more pressing matters to attend to,
like that throbbing love-missile Phil was pressing against my
stomach. I backed off and lowered my head to his huge cock.
This wasn't easy, but I finally got myself in position.

Phil was trembling as I put my mouth over his great cockhead. I teased it for a while as I licked, kissed and nibbled
on it. Then I ran my tongue along his shaft, pausing now
and then to suck his balls.

Liz must have been feeling left out, because she jumped
out of the hammock mumbling something about faggots. I
took Phil's rod out of my mouth to ask him if he felt like a
faggot. He laughed and told me to suck harder. I was really
getting into it, with my nose buried in Phil's pubic hair and
his cock halfway down my throat, so I don't know when
exactly Liz left. The next thing I knew, I heard the backdoor
slam and Phil said she'd gone inside. I didn't care.

Eventually Liz returned with a jar of honey. She said it
was time for lunch. I took Phil's cock out of my mouth and
asked her what she meant. Instead of answering me, she
caught hold of the hammock ropes and pulled us closer to
her. Then she tilted the jar and poured a thin stream of honey
over Phil's stomach. I watched, fascinated, as the golden
fluid pooled in his belly button and slowly rolled down his
upright cock. Tossing the empty jar aside, Liz stood on tiptoes
and leaned over this honey-coated feast. I joined in and,
together, we gave him a fabulous tandem blowjob.

When Phil grunted that he was about to come, Liz said
that she wanted to eat his come, so I started to lick his balls
as he came in Liz's mouth. Just then Liz lost her footing and
grabbed for the far side of the hammock. Her weight capsized
us and before I knew it, we were all in a pile on the grass
under the hammock. Phil's cock was still in her mouth and

from the way she was swallowing, I could tell he was still coming. At last Phil let out a low moan and collapsed on the grass. My wife grabbed his wilting stem around its base, slowly pulling its length from her mouth, and then licked him clean.

She gave me a kiss. I found out then that she had not swallowed all of Phil's come. She pushed some into my mouth and we shared it.

That was the end of a perfect day for all of us. It had also been an exhausting day. However, it was not the last that we spent together. We've never bothered with clothes since then, and Liz and Phil have free rein with each other whenever they want to, which is often. It isn't unusual for me to come home and find them fucking. Sometimes I just watch and at other times, I join in.

Phil and I also like to have sex together on occasion, and next weekend I'm going to help him hang a hammock in his backyard.

The Gift of Tongues

I was a mere eighteen years old then, and I have had many similar experiences since. But none were as memorable as this. I am a male, six feet six inches tall, and weighed only one hundred and eighty pounds back then. I have curly red hair, blue eyes and a lot of freckles all over my face, arms and shoulders. Not ugly, mind you; in fact I've been told so often that I am handsome that I am now convinced of it.

As I remember her, Molly was about five feet four inches tall, and maybe one hundred and five pounds, if that. She had chestnut-brown hair, cut in a short shag that was popular in the 1970s, with brown eyes to match. She had small but shapely breasts, and her womanly curves had not yet filled out completely.

One day not long after we started going together, Molly and I went up to the boardinghouse where I was living. At first we just sat on the sofa in the upstairs living room, cuddling and talking. Then I took her by the hand and led her to my room. My roommate Mark was at work in the shipyard, as were all of the other boarders, so we were all alone.

After closing the door, I turned to Molly and, not saying a word, bent over to give her a gentle kiss of reassurance. I felt her relax as my lips touched hers. I sat down on the edge of my bed and motioned for her to kneel on the floor in front of me, between my knees. Looking directly into her eyes, I very gently traced lines with my middle fingers of both hands, in small circles on her cheeks, spiraling outward until I reached her ears. I touched her small, slightly upturned nose, the flare of her nostrils, her lips. As my fingers caressed her lips. Molly began to rub her hands up and down my thighs.

I lifted her head to meet my lips and I kissed her. I kissed her gently, flicking my tongue lightly across her lips with short, brisk licks. I kissed her several times. As my tongue probed the inside of her mouth, finding her tongue and swirling around, I allowed my right hand to run down the front of her blouse till I reached the first button.

I deftly undid each button, gently drawing my finger along her flesh as it was exposed. When the last button was undone I removed her blouse, slipping it over her shoulders while keeping my lips pressed firmly to hers. Starting from her hands, which had reached up to grasp my shoulders, I ran my fingers along her arms to her neck. I caressed her shoulders, my hands meeting behind her neck.

Still kissing her, I unclasped her bra and let it dangle from her arms. I rubbed the flesh of her back where her bra had been, moving my hands up and over her shoulders and down to her firm little tits. I cupped those ripe peaches and gave them a gentle squeeze, running my thumbs over the nipples, feeling them grow erect with excitement.

When I finally ended our kiss, Molly was breathing heavy with excitement. "Wow!" she exclaimed. "Where on earth did you learn to kiss like that?"

I didn't say a word. I only smiled and lifted her to her feet. Looking up into her eyes once again, I undid the snap of her jeans and pulled down the zipper, all in one fluid motion.

With practiced ease, I peeled her jeans down over her

slender hips, inhaling the sweet aroma that assailed my nostrils from her dampening crotch.

Before removing the last piece of her clothing, I cupped the slight bulge that her pubic mound created in her panties. Her panties were soaking wet, and I could feel the heat emanating from her fiery slit.

My fingers shook in anticipation as I slid them up the front of her panties to grasp hold of the elastic waistband. Very slowly, I peeled Molly's panties down over her hips. Gazing up into her eyes, I reached around her and cupped her asscheeks, one in each hand, and bent forward to run the flat of my tongue along her dewy slit. Molly shuddered as my tongue made contact with her sensitive nubbin. She tasted even better than I had thought.

When I stood up, Molly climbed on the bed and lay down, motioning for me to come to her.

I positioned myself so that I was straddling her torso. I lowered my hips to where I could press my cock into her cunt, and leaned down to give her yet another gentle kiss. But this was not to be so, as Molly wrapped her arms around my neck, pulling herself up to me and firmly planting her lips on mine in a deep and very passionate soul kiss. I could hear her moan with desire as her tongue snaked out of her mouth into mine, dueling with it in a mad dance of sheer lust.

When she broke the kiss, Molly flopped down on the bed, breathing very heavily. "Do me!" she gasped. "Do my pussy! I need it so bad!"

I simply looked at her and smiled, but then moved down so I could use my tongue on her entire body. I slipped a knee between her tights so she could have something solid to hump on while I took care of her upper torso, slowly covering every square inch of her luscious flesh with my active tongue, being careful to avoid her temptingly hard nipples.

Finally, I flicked my tongue across the sensitive nubs,

causing her to buck and squirm beneath me. Molly was begging me to stop and move down to her honey-pot, which was soaking wet as it rubbed against my knee. I gave her nipples one last suck before moving down her belly with my tongue and lips. When I reached her navel, I stopped and began to lick circles around the deep depression. Molly raised her knees and used her hands on top of my head to try to push it down to her steaming snatch, but I simply stopped all tongue action until she realized that I was in control of the situation.

Spiraling inward, I dipped my tongue into the depths of her belly button, probing all around the inside. Molly gasped as my tongue found the bottom. She later told me that nobody had ever done this to her before. I guess not many people know the joys of navel sex.

From her navel, I then made my way down her groin to the brown triangle of Molly's pubic thatch. She began to hump her hips against my knee with an urgency that I found quite stimulating. I loved seeing her like this. Yet my aching cock still longed to plunge into the recesses of her fiery cunt. I could sense that she was near the brink of oblivion as I used my fingers to part the pouting petals of her juicy twat.

I gently tongued my way up one side of her outer labia, rounded the top of her slit and moved down the other side. I then dipped my talented tool into her honey-pot, wagging it back and forth, from side to side.

I could sense that Molly was getting closer, so I finally moved my mouth up to zero in on her visibly erect clitoris. The little nub glistened with her juices as I began to flick my tongue in circles around her button. Molly's breathing became ragged and short the nearer I licked. She began to churn her hips up to my face, trying to make the sensitive contact that would surely send her flying over the edge.

Finally I gave her that contact, but only briefly, teasing her to a fever pitch. She was begging me to tongue her clit, muttering obscenities in between gasps of air. I continued to tease her until she was frantic. And then I lay my tongue flat against her swollen clit, humming low in my throat. That was enough to do it. Molly went sailing off into outer space.

"Oh! . . . Oh, yes! . . . Yes! . . . That's it, lover!" she cried as she began the first series of powerful orgasms. "Eat it! Lick my cunt! Lick my pussy, motherfucker! Come! Coming! I'm . . . I'm . . . I'm coming!" Her body began to convulse uncontrollably with each racking wave of ecstasy.

"Oh baby! Baby . . . baby! . . . I love it!" she continued, as her head thrashed from side to side, her eyes tightly closed.

Molly continued to writhe in release as I alternately tongued her spasming clit and dipped into her clutching cunt. Her pussy was overflowing with fluid, and I did my best to lap it all up. When I returned to her joy button, Molly soared to even greater heights, grabbing me by the hair and mashing my face into her vulva. It was hard for me to breathe, but I didn't care because of the joy I was bringing to this delightful little creature.

After what seemed like an hour, she started to come back down to earth, releasing her grip on my head so I could come up for air. Once I got a lungful, I continued to tongue her cunt and returned to her clit to give it a gentle flick. Her whole body shook as a post-orgasmic tremor surged through her. I repeated this several times, shortening the interval between flicks of my tongue. Then I flattened my tongue against her vulva and began to wash it back and forth over her clitty. Molly responded with one long, shuddering, continuous convulsion.

Looking up at her, I saw that she had begun to cry. She explained that this was the first time she had ever come like that. Also, this was the first time she had really wanted to fuck but couldn't, because she was really shallow and small "down there." She said that whenever she tried, it caused her great pain, because she could not handle a normal-sized dick, let alone the monster that she imagined me to have.

I moved up to lie next to her, pulling her close to me and soothing her sadness. "Babes," I began, "my body may be long and lean, but Mother Nature has played a cruel joke on me."

"What do you mean?" she asked.

"This," I replied, getting off the bed to stand up and pull down my pants, revealing the slender six inches of cock that have been the cause of my learning to be so skilled with my fingers, tongue and lips.

"Oh, wow!" she exclaimed with delight, as she moved to the edge of the bed to face my throbbing member. "It's beautiful!" she added as she opened her mouth to engulf my entire shaft. Her cunt might have been shallow, but she sure had a deep throat.

Molly began to suck my steely rod with the earnestness of the well-loved. Her tongue swirled around it as she concentrated her attentions on the purple head, sending waves of pleasure coursing through my entire being. It didn't take much of this type of mouth action to bring me to a climax. She grabbed my ass and totally buried my cock in her sucking mouth.

With one hand, Molly grasped my dick around the base and began to jack it in time to her bobbing head while, with the other hand, she cradled my balls and began to squeeze gently.

With a stifled cry, I erupted in her adorable mouth, sending jet after powerful jet of white-hot semen splashing against the back of her throat. Molly just kept sucking and swallowing. She continued sucking until I had gone limp in her mouth, and then released it with a pop. Looking up at me for approval, I noticed a few droplets of sperm at the corners of her mouth, which she promptly licked off.

"Fan-fucking-tastic!" I sighed.

I never got to fuck Molly, although we stayed together for a couple of months after that. I know that I will always remember her with fondness and, even though the odds are against it, I keep hoping that someday we might meet again.

Private Showing

I am a twenty-two-year-old attractive blonde (five feet five at one hundred twenty pounds with blue eyes and a 34-22-34 figure) and happily married. I have never desired to sleep with another man since I have been married, and I have never been untrue to my husband. Until recently, that is.

One evening while my husband and I were lying naked in bed and cuddling, we began discussing our fantasies. My husband asked me what my most erotic and frequent fantasy was. I replied that I had always dreamed of making love to another woman. When I asked my husband to confess his most desirable fantasy, he replied that he often dreamed of watching me have sex with another man. I was a little shocked, but curious about what exactly he had fantasized.

He told me that his fantasies of me with another man did not include someone that we knew, but a stranger, someone who I would never see again and who would not threaten our marriage. While I played with his cock, I asked him to describe what he would like to see me do with another man. He did, and the evening ended as we straddled and made love.

I thought about his fantasy for the next week or so. At first the idea made me feel a little uncomfortable. However, I found myself thinking about it more and more and getting quite excited whenever I did. I soon found that whenever I would masturbate with my vibrator, I would fantasize about screwing another man. I love to masturbate with my vibrator, especially when my husband watches me. I usually start by gently rubbing and massaging my breasts until I get my nipples as erect as I can. Then I let my right hand slide down to my pussy, and I start to play with my inner lips. As my pussy begins to moisten, I slide my middle finger inside and get it wet so that I can easily rub my clit. As I start to approach orgasm, I take my vibrator, insert it and slowly slide it in and out. Then I quickly place the vibrator on my clit and explode into an orgasm. I can make myself come up to six or seven times when I use my vibrator, whereas I can only come once when my husband goes down on me.

It wasn't long before I told my husband that I would like for him to watch me make it with another man. He repeated that he did not want to see me make it with anyone we knew, but at the same time, we were both hesitant about getting a total stranger. Several weeks passed without anything else being said, until just prior to my birthday when my husband came home one evening and said that he had a plan. The plan would allow me to have sex with another very attractive man and, at the same time, allow us to remain complete strangers.

First, my husband called one of those singing telegram services and proceeded to tell them that, because he had to work late on my birthday, he would not be able to take me out as we had planned. He told them that in order to make it up to me, he wanted to hire a male stripper to come out to our house and sing "Happy Birthday" to me. He said I would be home alone, and that if the dancer explained who he was, I would let him in the house. On the night of my birthday and prior to the stripper's arrival, my husband instructed me to wear my short blue robe with nothing underneath. I placed some books on the couch so that it would appear that I was studying while waiting for my husband to come home.

As the time for my stripper's arrival neared my husband positioned himself in a closet that provided him with a clear view of our living room. When the doorbell rang, I answered it in a timid and cautious manner. The man explained who he was and who hired him, so I let him in, acting as if I had no idea what was going on. I excused myself for being dressed in only a robe and explained that I was getting ready to take a shower. I said, "If this isn't going to take long, I won't bother to get dressed."

He said, "It won't take long at all."

I led him into the living room and I sat on the edge of the chair. He had the entire room to dance and strip in front of me. He was by no means an average-looking man; he was the most gorgeous stud I had ever seen. He was six feet tall, had blue eyes, blond hair, broad, muscular shoulders, a washboard stomach and the tightest ass a girl could ask for. He had the facial features of a model and a smile that made me weak in the knees.

As he turned on his music and started to dance, I made sure that I was completely unexposed. He was wearing a karate outfit, and he seductively and sexily began to remove the karate belt. The top of his karate outfit fell open, and I was rewarded with my first glimpse of his handsome chest. He slowly danced over to me and lightly draped his karate belt around my neck as he leaned over to give me a small kiss on the lips. As he did so, I ran my hands up his chest. I was sure that by now my breasts were partly visible, as I was no longer making an effort to keep my robe closed. Next he danced back a step or two and removed his top, then his pants. He was now wearing only a pair of briefs. I could feel that not only were my nipples hard, but my pussy was so wet that the juice began to run down my crack. (This has only happened once or twice before in my life.)

He continued to dance for a while, turning around, enticing me with his sexy ass. He started to dance forward, bringing his crotch closer and closer. I finally reached out, cupped his beautiful ass with my hands and ran my tongue from the top of his underwear to his belly button. His bulge got noticeably larger. I asked him if he got that hard every time he stripped and he admitted he had never gotten a hard-on before while on the job. By now my robe was hanging open freely, and he took my hand, inviting me to dance with him. As I stood up and began dancing, he removed his briefs, exposing the skimpiest and sexiest G-string I have ever seen on a man. Seeing this, I removed my robe and began to dance closely next to him. His G-string barely covered what appeared to be a large and very attractive dick, which I could not wait to get my hands on.

There I was, dancing in the nude next to this gorgeous stranger dressed in only a G-string. The music ended and I stepped forward, put my arms around his neck and gave him a kiss. I could feel his hard-on pressing against my stomach, and a small drop of pussy juice began to run down my inner thigh. He stated that usually when he finishes stripping, the audience has on more clothes than he does, but that he enjoyed the change, I replied that I wasn't modest and that I was actually quite turned on. I asked if he would like something to drink as I turned and walked into the kitchen.

I poured him a glass of water, and as I was walking back into the living room, he was starting to put on his briefs. I said, "Wait, doesn't the birthday girl get to tip her stripper?"

He said, "Of course," and dropped his briefs on the floor. I went over to my robe, removed a ten-dollar bill from the pocket and walked over to him. I reached out with my left hand and pulled his G-string forward far enough so that I could get a good view. With my right hand, I slid the ten-dollar bill down and wrapped it around his balls. Then I slid my hand up to his dick and pulled it out of his G-string. I began to slowly stroke his large cock as I leaned forward to give him a long, passionate kiss. Our tongues eagerly began exploring each other's mouths. I continued to stroke his lovely cock as he put his arms around my naked body. I took my left hand and guided his hands down to my ass. He finally touched my soaking pussy. As he deftly played with it, I began stroking his cock faster and faster. We stopped kissing, and I whispered in his ear. "Please let me suck your cock. I want you to come in my mouth and then fuck my hot pussy."

He walked over to the couch and asked. "Do you always get this wet?"

I breathlessly replied, "I've never been this wet before in my life." I got down on my knees and slid his G-string all the way down. I asked him to sit on the couch, and I began to hungrily suck his cock like my life depended on it. With my right hand I began to feverishly rub my clit, but not for long because within minutes he began to unleash gobs of come down my throat. I was only able to swallow a little: the rest was smeared on my left hand and his cock. I took the come on my left hand and rubbed it all over my right tit and asked him to lick it off. He did promptly, going as far as savoring and swallowing his own juice.

We then lay on the couch together, kissing and exploring for the longest time. He kissed my neck while his hands massaged my breasts. I started to play with his limp dick and swollen balls. He moved his kisses lower until he was sucking my nipples. By now he had two fingers moving in and out of my pussy in a steady, continuous rhythm. His tongue ran down my stomach until his head was positioned between my legs. I was begging him to eat me out. He teased me by licking my inner thighs and running his tongue up the crack of my pussy. Next he began sucking my inner lips. I moaned in sheer ecstasy. It wasn't long before he was uncontrollably sucking my clit and darting his tongue in and out of my moist opening. It normally takes my husband ten to twenty minutes to make me come when he goes down on me, but this time I didn't last longer than five. I clenched his hair and tightly held his head between my legs as I ground my clit against his tongue. I came so much that I soaked the couch underneath my pussy. His mouth and chin were covered with my juice as he came up to kiss me on the lips. I was breathing heavy and had small red patches on my chest. I stuck my tongue into his mouth and tasted myself, rubbing my jutting clit all the while.

As we were kissing, I reached down and guided his cock into my hot pussy. He moved in and out slowly, increasing his rhythm. I was meeting each of his thrusts with my rising hips. He continued his hard, driving jabs for what seemed an eternity until he finally exploded with a shuddering orgasm. I felt his come running out of my pussy and trailing down the crack of my ass. Finally, he collapsed on top of me and we lightly kissed. We lay there quietly until his limp dick gradually slipped out of my hole.

After a little while I said it would be a good idea if he left, since I was expecting my husband home soon. I lay back and relaxed as he got dressed. I walked him to the door. We French-kissed deeply and then said good-bye. As he left, he gave me his card and asked me to call him if I ever needed his services again. With a smile, I told him I sure would.

After the stripper left, I went back into the living room and found my husband waiting for me on the couch, completely naked. I approached him and stood in front of him.

He sat up and began to massage my pussy, which still had some come inside it. He sucked on my right nipple as I held his head firmly at my breast. My husband sat back on the couch, and I positioned my pussy over his mouth. He gently parted my pussy lips with his fingers, and his tongue began to caress the inside of my pussy. He was supporting my ass with the palms of his hands as I moved back and forth on his tongue. Finally, he began sucking on my clit and fingering my hole. It took me longer than usual, but eventually I shuddered with my second orgasm of the evening. He continued swabbing my clit with his tongue.

I then sat back and slid my husband's hard dick into my moist pussy. He was extremely excited, yet able to last for what seemed a lifetime as I moved up and down on his stiff dick. My husband seemed to fuck me with more vigor that night than ever before. He continued to fuck me until finally he shot the largest load of come ever into my wet pussy. We both collapsed in exhaustion. Then, sheened in sweat, we fell asleep. It was the finest birthday present ever, and I have been devising ways to make my husband's next birthday as exciting as mine was.

Trivial Pursuit

My wife stands five feet three and weighs about one hundred and twenty pounds. Her measurements are 34-28-35, and she knows how to move every succulent inch when we make love. She has big, brown eyes and a tantalizing smile that never fails to draw men's attention.

I am six feet tall, weigh about two hundred and thirty-five pounds, have dark brown curly hair and the same color eyes. My vital statistics, for those who may be interested, are: chest, 50; shoulders, 54; waist, 38. I have an average-size cock. My wife and I keep in shape by being active in various sports, such as volleyball, tennis and, for my wife, a Nautilus health center.

The incident I want to describe occurred last year when Lisa, then twenty-six, and I, then twenty-eight, were trying to conceive our first child. After figuring out when conception would be most likely for her, Lisa devised some kinky escapades to get things rolling. Well, after a few months of trying, she still wasn't pregnant. I told her that the next month would be mine to plan. She was to leave everything in my hands. Lisa somewhat reluctantly agreed (I am known for my kinky imagination). I assured her I'd try not to get too out of hand.

As the weekend approached, I came up with a suitable plan for some good fun and games.

I wanted to make this as unforgettable as I could. On Saturday I told Lisa to be ready by eight that evening. I asked her to keep an open mind, which I knew wouldn't be difficult because Lisa's pretty open-minded as it is. That's what helps to keep our marriage going. As eight drew near, she said she was going to take a shower and get ready. As soon as she was in the shower, I jumped into our van and sped to the nearby market. I purchased a can of whipped cream and then went to the local video store to rent some X-rated movies. I picked up three we had never seen before. I hurried back to our apartment with plenty of time to spare. I placed one of the tapes into the VCR and fast-forwarded to the first sex scene. I shut the machine off and hid the other two tapes and the whipped cream so Lisa wouldn't see them. Next I took out our favorite toy, a seven-inch vibrator, and hid it in the living room. I placed a couple of blankets on the floor in front of the television.

Lisa finished her shower and went into the bedroom to change. She was strutting around with the most devilish smile I'd ever seen. She was curious, but also a little leery of my imagination. When she said she was ready, I told her we were going to play one of her favorite board games, Trivial Pursuit. Only this time the rules were going to be slightly different. If you missed an answer, you had to remove a piece of clothing, and when you no longer had any clothing left, you had to do whatever the other person said for five minutes. She was a little hesitant about the last stipulation, but decided to go along with it, anyway. I thought for sure that I was going to literally lose my shirt since Lisa is so good at this game, but, instead, it was Lisa who couldn't think of the answers. First, off came the socks. Then the sweats to reveal my favorite black-and-red-trimmed teddy underneath. I got hard seeing how her nipples pressed against the fabric of the teddy. When she lost the next round, she slowly stood up, reached between her legs, and unsnapped the snaps. She wiggled out of her teddy, bending toward me and smiling, and revealed another bikini. She looked so sexy I almost shot a load right there in my pants. When she stood straight up, her breasts wiggled so succulently that my mouth watered. I almost felt like saying the hell with the rest of the game and screwing her right then and there.

I lost the next five rounds straight and was down to my bikini underwear. Lisa lost the next round and removed her bikini to expose another bikini. This was the skimpiest thing I had ever laid eyes on. By then, I was lusting for her like a schoolboy in heat.

I lost the next two rounds and stood before Lisa with one mother of a big hard-on. It wasn't difficult to notice that she was also excited. Her nipples were jutting and her areolae were all puckered up, waiting to be sucked. Lisa was delighted when she noticed I had trimmed my pubic hair and had shaved my balls. She smiled and said, "Ummm," slowly running her tongue over her lips.

Lisa lost her next turn. She stood up and moved seductively over to my side of the table, turned her back to me, and bent over invitingly as she pulled down her panties. She wiggled her cute little ass and looked over her shoulder to watch as I ogled her. She straightened up and turned around to display her pussy, which had been shaved to form a cute triangle. The next round Lisa lost again, and for the next five minutes I had her French-kissing me with her beautiful, full lips. With her tongue, she slowly moved down my chest, stomach and, finally, my cock. She ran her tongue up and down the underside of my shaft, then she stuffed the entire length into her mouth. One thing about my lover, she *loves* to give head, and, believe me, nothing beats a woman who enjoys what she is doing.

I lost the next round, and my beautiful little wife instructed me to lick and suck her breasts. She loves when I do this. She moaned and shivered with pleasure as I feasted on her soft globes.

After I finished with her tits, we played another round. She won again. She lay back on the couch with her ass propped on the edge of the ottoman and her legs open slightly, just enough for me to see her tight little nook.

She had me suck and kiss her whole body, but I had strict orders not to touch her pussy. This drove me crazy. It drove her crazy, too. I could smell that special aroma that comes from a woman when she's aroused. It drove me wild. I won the next round and had her sit on the floor with her back against the couch. I told her to watch the video on the television as I caressed her breasts and nibbled her ear. She was moaning as we watched the couple humping and slurping on the screen.

The next round was mine again. We repeated the previous scene, only this time she was to caress her own breasts and finger her own stiff little clit. To my enjoyment, the next scene on the video was a threesome, with two men fucking and sucking the same woman. I especially enjoyed this scene since I've often fantasized about having a threesome with me, my wife and another man. By the end of the five minutes, Lisa's juices were all over her hands and inner thighs.

The next few rounds involved the can of whipped cream. We covered each other with it and then took turns greedily lapping it off. I had avoided Lisa's clitoris. I knew if I concentrated on that delicious, protruding button too much, she would go off like a firecracker. But now it was time for my real surprise. When Lisa lost the next round, I had her lie on the blankets and I started the VCR. I then brought out the vibrator, and she looked at me sultrily with her brown eyes. I turned on the seven-inch vibrator, which we had nicknamed Pierre. It hummed softly. I ran it all over her body. First, I had her lie on her stomach, facing the television so she could watch the action while enjoying the massage. I moved Pierre along her neck and shoulders, then I slowly moved our friend down to the small of her back. Slowly, I moved the vibrator down over her succulent buttocks, down her legs to her feet. After spending some time on her feet and calves, I ever so slowly brought Pierre up her thighs to her firm cheeks. Tenderly, I began to knead and massage them. Then, to her surprise, I ran Pierre along the crack of her ass. When I spread her legs, I could hear the moist smacking of her gorgeous, inner lips parting. Kissing her neck, shoulder and back, I moved Pierre down the crack of her ass and along her pussy lips. With each passing stroke, Lisa would let out short gasps and moans. I had her turn over. We repositioned ourselves in a 69 so that my blood-engorged cock was hoisted directly over her moist, inviting lips, and I had a close-up view of her nicely trimmed, soaking pussy.

I went back up to her chest and ran the vibrator over her edible little nipples and then back down to her pubic mound. This time as I moved near my wife's delicious pussy, she took hold of my cock and began to lick and suck my shaft and balls. When Pierre reached Lisa's thighs, she parted them ever so slightly, releasing once again that intoxicating aroma of her womanhood. Her pussy was wetter than I had ever seen. She was drenched with her own juices. I took Pierre and began to slowly massage around her pubic area. Then I moved down to her swollen outer lips, still avoiding her clitoris. Lisa gasped and squeezed my cock with her mouth as I slid Pierre back and forth from her pussy lips to her creamy thighs. This drove her crazy. During all of this, I began to talk to her about having another man here to help please her. Even though she gets upset at me when I bring this up any other time, while I was gently rubbing her pussy with the vibrator, she became really turned on.

By now her moaning had drowned out the action coming from the television. While Lisa was sucking and fondling my cock and balls, I began to slowly apply more and more pressure until the vibrating head of Pierre disappeared inside her slick confines. Slowly, tenderly, inch by inch, I moved Pierre in and out of her. With each stroke, she moaned and gasped for air, yet she never released my cock from the warm, soft confines of her mouth. Soon I began to feel the familiar tingling in my balls. As I continued moving Pierre in and out of her, I began to finally lick and nibble on her gorgeous clit. It was sticking out so much that it looked like a small penis. She frantically gobbled my cock while my intense tonguing brought her to the verge of climaxing. Then I slowly moved the soaking vibrator out of Lisa and turned to face her. She was flushed and her eyes radiated with pure lust.

I pulled her on top of me into one of our favorite positions, and I slid right into her soft, velvety interior.

We began to French-kiss and caress each other as we moved toward our impending climaxes. Her pussy juice was dripping down my balls. She sat straight up and started rocking back and forth while caressing her own breasts. My cock felt like it was going to explode. I began to rub her body with my hands. The look of pure pleasure on Lisa's face was one that I'll never forget. She lowered herself so I could suck on her luscious tits. I moved my hands down and began to squeeze the firm globes of her tantalizing ass. She was so drenched with juice that the entire crack was as slippery as her lovecanal.

She slipped up and down on my cock and rubbed her tits against my chest. She went over the edge and climaxed with the strongest orgasm that she had ever experienced. I was right behind her. I slid my throbbing shaft all the way into her inner recesses as I climaxed and pumped my juice deep inside her. She and I lay side by side, facing each other, hugging and kissing, saying how much we loved one another.

It was nine months later that Lisa gave birth to our first beautiful baby girl.

The Best Medicine

Toward the end of World War II, I came home from Europe with several wounds and decorations. After a lengthy stay in the hospital I was granted a recuperation leave. I decided to spend a few weeks with two old-maid aunts who lived some fifty miles away on the edge of a very small town. It was very healthy with the fresh air and all.

In the same town there lived two girls with their family, one twenty and the other eighteen. The younger was very pretty and away at school. The older, Pam, was not that pretty, being a bit on the masculine side. She spent a lot of time at my aunts'. They had a horse she liked to ride.

One day I was in the barn getting ready to jack off. I was sitting on a bench, leaning against a stall, my hard dick in my hand. Pam walked in just then. She stopped halfway, stared at my dick and slowly walked over to me. I asked her to have a seat. She said she had never seen a hard-on before.

Embarrassed. I slipped my cock back into my pants. I started up a conversation to relieve the tension in the air. She talked about her complete lack of social life, how she never had any dates. She was depressed all the time, and didn't know what to do about it.

I told her that what she needed was an education in human relations. She agreed. I suggested she come to the house the next day. I knew my aunts would be out of town. Right away she seemed very interested and agreed to come over.

Sure enough, my aunts weren't gone five minutes and she came over. She seemed a bit nervous, and I made jokes to try and relax her a bit. I chose the front bedroom so we would be able to hear if anyone came around.

We went in, closed the door and pulled down the shades. She sat on the bed, a very apprehensive look on her face. I pulled off my shirt, shoes and pants, leaving on only my undershorts. I sat next to her and started to unbutton her shirt. When I got to the last button she stopped my hands and took a deep breath. I knew I'd better slow down or I'd scare her away. I spent some time kissing her and gently massaging her back, loosening her up. After a few minutes of that she didn't try to stop me as I slipped her shirt off her body, seeing her very small breasts.

I leaned over, moistened my lips with my tongue and kissed her on the mouth. She moaned. I kissed her again, longer, harder, opening my mouth slightly. As she responded to my kisses, I undid her bra. I flicked my tongue over her lower lip. She responded by opening her mouth and letting the tip of her tongue touch mine. She was getting into it now as I slipped her bra off, revealing breasts the size of small oranges, with very large nipples.

By this time my dick was hard and poking out of my shorts. Very gently I pushed her down on the bed so her feet were dangling over the side. I moved up and started kissing her again. Very soon she had opened her mouth and was receiving my tongue and giving me some of hers. I pulled away from her and started on her breasts. She couldn't take much of this before she started rolling and bucking on the bed. I moved my head down to her thigh and started working my way up to her pussy. By the time my hand reached her crotch, she was shaking.

I got up. I unbuttoned her shorts and, in one motion, pulled them and her panties off. She lay before me, a virgin waiting for whatever came next. I started rubbing her body, never once touching her pussy. She had long, strong, slender legs, a flat stomach and a small bush of black hair. My kisses started again. I worked my way up to her pussy, once again not touching it. By the time I got there she was a bundle of rolling, rocking, feminine spasms. Finally she asked me to touch her, which I proceeded to do with first my fingers, then with my tongue. She orgasmed and let out a high-pitched scream that should have brought the police. Not only had she never been sucked before, this was her first orgasm. She freely admitted to having rubbed her pussy a few times, but she had always stopped well short of climax.

After she had rested we started talking about what we had done. She was still a virgin and my dick was still very hard. I asked her to jerk me off, all the while explaining to her what was going to happen. She was fascinated with the prospect. I took over just before shooting and directed my come onto her naked thighs. She was delighted with having my semen all over her. I told her it was all protein. I got some on my finger and sucked it down. I asked her to do the same. She did, evidently liking it.

I put my dick, still very erect, into her mouth. She took it willingly and proceeded to suck on it. It wasn't long before I was once again shooting, and she took all of it, giving a little of it back to me in a kiss.

This ended the first day of her "schooling" but not her education. A short while later I popped her cherry, and we were soon fucking regularly. I also showed her how to 69. The only problem was whenever she came she'd really scream her head off. We always had to fool around in out-of-the-way places to avoid being found out.

Then she moved away to the city. I saw her again, five years after our affair had come to an end. She told me she was living with a beautiful young woman who was her lover.

So much for modern education.

Clean and Supple

While touring the western Pacific as a U.S. marine, I encountered numerous exotic playthings that greatly inspired my lust for the erotic. Even though each was outstanding in her own way, one *sensei* (master) allowed me, her young pupil, a brief glimpse into the window of pure eroticism. Travel through southeast Asia was no new experience, considering I'd spent the better part of my twenty-two years growing up in third-world countries.

Our ship had been anchored off of Pattaya, Thailand, for four days when my friend Carl and I decided to take a much-needed break from all the drinking and carousing. We were searching for a nice, secluded massage parlor when we stumbled upon the fabled "Sabailand."

Our resident expert guided us through a maze of candle-lit tables and nude statues. We turned a corner in the parlor and I felt my lungs constrict sharply as my eyes viewed the most incredible sight I had ever seen. Of course, my lungs weren't the only part of my anatomy to respond to the vision before me. There, separating me from Valhalla, were three plate-glass windows. Behind the windows, in various colorful stages of undress, were seventy-five of the prettiest women I'd ever seen. Discs numbered from seven to two hundred fifty-nine were pinned on the girls' fishnet bikini bottoms and elaborate silk teddies, which barely left anything to the imagination. I hastily asked our guide if he could bring me a glass of native beer while I regained my composure and scanned the faces and bodies for the one girl that would satisfy my intense hunger.

After I finished my beer, I'd made my decision. Upon my request the guide walked up to the windows and, through an intercom, requested that number two hundred twenty-six relinquish her spot on the carpeted dais and meet her new customer. After allowing us only to exchange a mere few words and names with the ladies of our choice, the guide whisked Carl and me up an elevator to the third floor.

With a twist of a key and a flick of a switch I entered what could have only been a dream. In front of me was a large tile floor which led to a deep bathtub on my right. On my left was a massage table. As I imagined what was going to happen to me on the table, I felt a tap on my shoulder. In sexy, broken English, my little demigoddess explained that I was to undress and climb into the tub of soothing hot water. She laid down the air mattress she had brought in with her and slipped slowly out of her clothes to reveal her perfectly shaped breasts, supple waist and long slender legs.

I, too stunned to be at all embarrassed, saw the engorged head of my member protruding above the water while she commenced cleaning every inch of my body, paying close attention to my erogenous zones. Not a part of me was left unnoticed or untouched.

Next, she bade me to lie down on the air mattress while she concocted her mystical Asian potion. She had filled a basin with warm water and dumped a dozen or so bars of soap into it. Then she added a final, mysterious ingredient and then whipped up mounds of billowy, strawberry-smelling suds that she heaped upon my yearning body and hers.

Thus slicked down, she slid her body up and down my back while using her hands to further her massaging expertise. What followed were a myriad of yoga-type movements that left no doubt in my mind that she truly was a professional. Placing one muscular leg under my body and clamping down with the other, she massaged my legs and loins with hers, leaving me breathless, relaxed and eager for more.

I then rolled over so that she was straddling me. Placing her hands on my shoulders she ground the insides of her thighs and her perfectly mounded mons up my involuntarily tightening stomach, over the crest of my chest and up higher.

As she resumed this motion back down my torso and onto my thighs I knew she was reaching that incredible crescendo. With her head thrown back and a low, earthy moan emitting from her lips she grasped my straining cock as if she were pulling herself out of the grip of a raging whirlpool. She seemingly tried to pull herself hand over hand up my rigid pole only to slide down again due to the soapsuds. Again and again she attempted this maneuver until she felt the cauldrons start to boil. Then, through half-closed eyelids and semiconsciousness, I realized she had stopped and was beckoning me to climb into the tub once again, where she rinsed off our soapy bodies.

And then, while I waited what seemed an agonizingly cruel eternity, she toweled us dry and led me by the hand to the massage table. When she beckoned me to lie down, I realized that I would soon turn to jelly if I let her massage me any more. I refused and gently but firmly laid her down on the table.

Slowly spreading her supple thighs. I knelt poised—like a warrior preparing his coup de grâce on some fallen enemy—

over her gaping vagina, slickened now with more than just soapsuds. And with more energy than a tiger leaping on its prey, I plunged into her waiting depths. My pulsating pillar of manhood showed no mercy, having been denied its just reward for so long, as I thrust in and out of those gripping walls . . .

. . . And as the fireworks of the two hundred and tenth July Fourth blinded me, she screamed the voice of thousands caught in the path of an erupting volcano, as my lavalike semen coursed through her womb.

I'm on my way back to Thailand in four months and can't wait to see my *sensei* again. There's nothing like a really good bath.

Overexposed

One sunny Saturday, my morning was filled with errands. My last stop was a pet store specializing in exotic animals, to buy food for my Amazon parrot. I purchased the seed and asked the young man at the front counter about a problem I was having with my bird, who seemed to be losing his pep. The man directed me to the back of the store, where another, more knowledgeable clerk was working.

I saw a slender young redhead sitting on a stool in the back room, with a large white rabbit in her lap. Her bright green eyes were astounding, her smile radiant. Her natural red curls, with just the faintest golden highlights, softly framed her angelic face. She was a tiny creature, and looked so sweet sitting there, petting her furry white bunny.

I explained my parrot's problem to her, and she asked me a few questions. She said I needed to pay more attention to him—to give him special treats and sing to him. She was friendly, so we began to talk at length about our mutual love for birds. I noticed two excellent, extremely well-lit photographs of exotic birds on the wall. When I admired them, she gave credit to her boyfriend, Toby, who she said was a professional photographer.

"Does he ever photograph people?" I asked.

"Quite often," she replied. "I've modeled for him many times."

"I'm considering having some nude photographs of myself taken," I said. "I'd like a memento for my old age, and I won't look like this forever." I'm twenty-nine and have a terrifically sinuous body that I've always been quite proud of. I stand five feet five inches, have natural blonde shoulder-length hair, an ample bustline, a twenty-five-inch waistline, and I weigh one hundred and sixteen pounds.

I continued to converse with the comely redhead, and she gave me her boyfriend's business card and insisted that I call him. We smiled and waved good-bye, and I took a lingering look at her standing in the doorway. Beneath her thin cotton blouse she was braless. The rays of sunlight streaming in surrounded her creamy, flawless skin as if it were an aura, making her appear even more angelic.

That evening, at a drive-in, in my boyfriend Marc's car, I explained to him my desire to have some nude photos taken of myself. I unzipped his pants and rubbed his cock gently, teasing his balls with my fingertips. Marc has a masterful cock. He's also an expert at cunnilingus. He moaned as I ran my tongue along the ridges of his cock and over its head. When I described the little redhead from the pet shop to him, he got really hard. Right through my tight blouse, he placed his lips over my left nipple and sucked at it. He told me that having the photos done was a great idea, but he wanted to come along to watch.

"I want to make sure that Toby doesn't get the wrong idea," he said.

"I wouldn't have it any other way," I replied, teasing.

He reached under my blouse and unsnapped my bra, freeing my breasts. He then lifted my skirt and, with his usual precision, slipped his roaring engine into me. I trembled and came instantly—we hadn't been together for almost a week. Marc took his time and continued to stroke me slowly, like a pro. But then the second feature started and we wanted to watch it, so he licked and nipped at my erect nipples until I came a second time. He plunged his engine even deeper into my wet pussy before he exploded wildly.

I waited a day before calling Toby. He sounded professional and enthusiastic on the phone, so we set a date for a photo shoot the following Saturday, and he gave me his address.

When Saturday rolled around, Marc and I drove to the address Toby had given me. It was a large duplex apartment along a cul-de-sac in a wholesome suburban neighborhood. The redhead answered the door when we knocked, and introduced herself.

"Hi, I'm Audrey. We didn't get around to introductions when we met in the store last week."

"Nice seeing you again, Audrey. I'm Gina, and this is Marc."

"Welcome, both of you," she beamed, and opened the door to let us in.

She walked barefoot across the plush navy rug. The furniture was all white and soft beige. She wore cutoffs, and a hint of her round, white ass was visible. She told us to have a seat and said she'd be back in a minute with something cold to drink. When she turned to leave the room, I noticed Marc's eyes following her, sizing her up seductively.

"She's even better looking than you described," he said carefully.

"Almost supernatural," I said to myself, wondering if I should have left Marc home.

I may have been imagining this, but when she returned with our drinks, it looked as if another button on her blouse was undone. She was wearing a thin cotton blouse similar to the one she had been wearing when I first met her, but this time I could clearly see the texture and color of her small red nipples sticking up underneath. She was dressed very provocatively for one with such an angelic aura, which only made her more intriguing.

"Why don't we go into the studio? It's cozy there too," she said in a relaxed voice.

There was one black wall and one white wall in the photography studio. Equipment was set up in the far corner. Toby turned and smiled at us, but was busy adjusting the lights, so he didn't say anything. Huge, overstuffed black-and-white pillows were scattered all over the floor. Audrey plopped down on one of them and patted the pillows on either side of her.

"Have a seat. Relax. Toby likes to combine his photo sessions with a party atmosphere. You'll get much better pictures if you're not nervous," she explained. She lit up a joint and passed it to me. "I think you'll appreciate a few tokes of this," she said.

"I'll be okay," I said as I took a hit. "I've had more medical students gawking at me in my gynecologist's office."

I passed the joint back to Audrey. Toby moved in front of me with his camera and said to me softly, "Take your clothes off now, okay? Or would you like to do some poses half-clothed?"

"That would be nice, but this is all I have on," I answered, and lifted my form-fitting jersey dress over my head. I never wear underwear, and had on only a single garter and high heels.

Audrey and Marc sat down together in the corner. I began to pose, first lying down, then sitting in a ladylike manner. But Toby walked over to me, tapped my knees so that my legs fell open and quickly took a shot of my snatch.

"Those aren't the kind of shots I had in mind," I said, shocked.

"That was just for fun," he laughed.

Then he took pictures of my naked body from many angles—shots from behind as I knelt or stood, and side views of my breasts and erect nipples. Then I got down on all fours and he took close-ups of my tits from every imaginable angle. I wet my finger and rubbed it over the tips of my nipples to make them glisten. We were having so much fun that we barely noticed that Marc had taken Audrey's shirt off and was playing with her tits.

When Toby asked me to stand up for some full frontal shots, I instantly froze. So he said to Audrey, "Could you break it up there for a minute and help her with this?"

Audrey walked over to me slowly and pulled my body close to hers, kissing me on the lips. When she tongued my mouth I put my arms around her. She reached down and placed her delicious lips on my tit, while I reached for her pointed breasts and perky nipples, which were still warm from Marc's hot hands. I helped her take off her panties, then rubbed my hand over her furry little box. I sucked luxuriously on one hardening nipple while gently holding her other breast in my hand. We rubbed our pussies together to excite each other's clit.

Audrey put her hand between my legs and fingered my slit. She opened my red-hot pussy lips with her thumb and little finger, and tapped her middle finger erratically against my slippery flesh. She slid her finger into my pussy while she pulled my pleasure orbs to her mouth and sucked them like a hungry little kitten. We sank onto the pillows, and she held her sweet-smelling snatch open so that I could explore it with my lips and tongue.

I had eaten pussy only once before, but I rolled my tongue

in circles around her hot box and licked her clitoris until it glistened. Suddenly I sensed how steamy the room was getting. Toby was frantically snapping photos, and when I looked over at Marc, I saw that he had taken off all his clothes. His penis was standing straight out, and though I've deep-throated him many times, I had never seen his virile instrument this huge before. As he watched Audrey run her smooth fingers over my body, he began to stroke himself impatiently. She leaned toward me and ran her tongue along my belly up to my chest, where she sucked fervently on each of my nipples. It felt great.

Marc approached us as I reclined on the pillows. Audrey's fiery mouth was still sucking away at my tit, where she contented herself until my nipple and her lips seemed to be one. I cupped my hands around her breasts and gently shook them; the shimmying made her nipples even harder. I noticed Marc's eyes on her tight little ass and I thought he was going to fuck her from behind. I would have loved to watch him fuck her doggie-style while she and I kissed and fondled one another. But instead, Marc joined Audrey, sucking my other breast into his mouth.

Suddenly, Marc and Audrey were locked in an embrace, French-kissing passionately. I took this opportunity to slide between Audrey's legs again. With my tongue I parted the silky, golden-red curls of her pretty pussy lips and let my teeth glide over her throbbing clitoris. I sucked deeply until I was light-headed. When I looked up, I saw that they were still kissing, and Marc was massaging her supple white tits with his beautifully tanned hands.

She lowered herself to kiss my eyelids, then said, "I want to get a better look at Marc's cock. I think we've been neglecting him."

When her attractive green eyes beheld his huge cock, she gasped. She grabbed his cock with her long, feminine fingers, put her lips over the head of it and began to coax him with her experienced tongue. I ran my hands over her smooth, pear-shaped bottom and patted her pussy with my hand. All this while, Toby was having a field day with his zoom lens but, to tell you the truth, we were barely aware of him.

Audrey energetically slid her lips up and down Marc's massive cock. I was amazed—her mouth almost doubled in size, but she never broke stride. She seemed happy and eager to be the perfect sucking machine. I wondered if he had ever been inside a pussy that felt that good. Unmercifully, I tickled his balls with my tongue until he pleaded, "No, no. Please, no."

He didn't want it to end yet, so I let go of his gems and sampled Audrey's luscious tit again. She was sweeter each time I tasted her.

Toby couldn't handle it any longer. He dragged me away from Audrey, laid me on the floor and began licking my pussy. He thrust his tongue in and out, and jiggled my protruding clit back and forth. He paid attention to every inch. His hands and tongue were a tormenting mixture of smoothness and roughness, and I closed my eyes, feeling as if I were drifting into outer space.

When I opened my eyes, I saw the full length of Marc's rigid cock still sliding in and out of Audrey's mouth. Her hands clutched his perfectly hard ass as he guided her back and forth over his slippery erection. She was making lovely sucking sounds, and I thought she would come simply from the pulse of his excited cock in her mouth. But Marc wanted his turn, so he spread her legs wide and buried his head between them. Opening her labia with his fingers, he searched for hidden treasure with his magnificent tongue. He licked and sucked her seam until, from the sounds she made, it was clear that she was having one orgasm after another, each one more intense than the last.

When Toby heard her impassioned cries, he slipped his tool inside me and moved it back and forth provocatively. The ridges of his powerful cock filled every crevice of my vagina. He plunged in deeper, then smiled as he took my breasts in his hands and squeezed them together. The come gushed from me, while Marc, ignoring Audrey's pleas, poked his tongue deeper into her pussy. She threw her head from side to side in ecstasy. Toby gave another thrust and then exploded. Come spurted from his pulsating penis in a seemingly endless flow.

Marc, who always has to have the last word, decided it was a good time to satisfy himself. Toby picked up his camera again, setting the shutter for fast action. Marc lifted Audrey and sat her on his perpendicular cock. He held her there, and she wrapped her long legs around his firm body. Her pussy was in spasms. He bounced her up and down on his hot tool for a few minutes and kissed her creamy white throat. Then they rolled to the floor still entwined. Marc held on to Audrey's waist and lifted her up and down on his smoking cock. I thought they were going to spontaneously combust. Suddenly, Marc shot his juice into her lovely pussy, and their bodies shook with pleasure—her tiny frame strained against his enormous member. She collapsed on top of him, and he fondled her gorgeous white ass. Toby finally ran out of film and we all sat there together, happy, naked and spent, and lit up another joint.

Audrey, Marc and I would like to plan another party like this—if Toby ever comes out of the darkroom.

In Concert

I recently went to a large outdoor concert with my boyfriend, Mitch. There were supposed to be about fifty thousand people there, but judging by the way we were crunched together I'm sure there were a lot more. It was a hot summer night, so I wore a miniskirt with no underwear and a loose-fitting T-shirt that did its best to hide my braless, 36C breasts. We were standing about a hundred feet from the stage, packed like sardines.

Once the music started, we all began swaying to the beat and singing along. Suddenly I felt something in my hair, and I quickly turned around to see what it was. When I did, I was startled to meet the most stunning green eyes I've ever seen in my life. They belonged to an absolute hunk. I froze for a moment, overtaken by his looks. He was wearing no shirt and only a tight pair of jeans. His short dark hair, combined with his tan, muscular body, sent a chill all the way down to my cunt. The unmistakable bulge in his jeans didn't help matters. I quickly turned around because I was beginning to blush and didn't want him to see.

I kept taking short glances behind me, and soon realized those incredible eyes were constantly on me instead of the stage. The crowd had started to shift, and my boyfriend was in front of me and to the side, with people standing between us. The sun slipped down soon after and left a giant full moon hanging above the large stage. My mystery man got more courageous as night fell.

While dancing to the music, I felt him moving against me in unison to the beat. Since I didn't move away, he must have thought I approved. Not that there was much room to move in anyway. I could feel his bulge grinding against my ass-cheeks as we rocked back and forth. I was a bit nervous with my boyfriend only four feet away. But whenever Mitch turned around he could only see my head, so I really didn't have to worry. Believe me, it's not like me to do something like that, but the wetness between my legs was driving me crazy. If only the guy hadn't been so hot, I would've been able to control myself.

When I peeked around again, I saw my mystery man mouth the words, "You're beautiful." Again, I turned away, blushing. He never stopped his grinding. Then he reached under my T-shirt from behind and played with my back and sides. I was so into it at that point, I began pushing my ass back against his solid cock. As he felt my approval, his hands started tickling my stomach, just below my bare tits.

I was too shy to touch him, but I knew he needed no encouragement. He removed his hands from my stomach for a few seconds. Then I felt his bare cock rubbing against me. He took my hand and placed it under the front of my miniskirt. I felt his cock poking through my legs from behind. I separated my thighs a bit so he could rub his long shaft against my soaked cunt. During all this, my boyfriend kept looking over at me. I'd smile and he'd go right back to watching the concert. Little did he know . . .

My secret stud had put his hands back inside my shirt and was lightly rubbing the tender underside of my tits. I was holding his cock, rubbing the shaft against my pussy lips. Soon I could feel my first orgasm arriving as his large head slid over my fiery clit. My body shook as he lightly held my breasts and, with his thumb and index finger, rolled my fully erect nipples like a radio dial. I did my best to control my gripping orgasm. As it subsided, Mitch looked over at me. He must have thought something was wrong, because he made his way through the crowd and over to me.

I panicked for a second, throwing the stranger's hands off my body. His cock was still hard and touching my cunt. I tried to move forward but he grabbed my hips and held me there. Mitch stood right in front of me and asked if everything was all right. I quickly said, "Yes. Why?" He said I looked like I was in pain or something. I told him not to worry and enjoy the show like I was.

While I was talking to my boyfriend, the hunk behind me had grabbed the swollen base of his cock and was searching for the opening to my pussy. I closed my legs, knowing if he found it I would be powerless to conceal my pleasure, and my boyfriend would discover us. I had to ask Mitch to turn around so I could rest my hands on him. He turned and I grabbed his hips. At the same time, I moved my ass farther back to accommodate the stranger's prick. Everyone was so close, there was no way anyone could have seen us. I felt him lift the back of my skirt up over my ass. He then took some time to massage me.

I was so wet I had no trouble accepting his large tool when he finally penetrated me from behind. I pushed back until he was all the way inside. His cock was much bigger than my boyfriend's. It brought me pleasures I'd never known before. The group started playing their most popular song and everyone went wild. Mitch thought my screams were for the band. He turned around to tell me what a great show it was. All I could reply was that it was the best. What I really meant was the giant cock pounding into me from behind!

My stranger had a tight hold on my hips and was working his cock in and out of me with absolute expertise. I could do nothing to hide my screams as orgasm after orgasm coursed through me. Mitch turned around in the middle of one of them and began kissing me, still not suspecting a thing. I stuck my tongue into his mouth. The sensation of having a complete stranger's dick up my cunt while French-kissing my boyfriend, who had no way of knowing what was going on, was one that I'm sure I will never forget. Mitch broke our kiss and said I was making him horny, and that he was going to give me the fucking of my life when we got home after the show. I said I had everything I needed right there with me, referring, of course, to the fuck-machine behind me, who hadn't let up during our entire conversation.

Mitch smiled and said, "You naughty girl, we can't do that here." That was enough. I turned him around and told him to enjoy the last part of the show. It took all I had to keep my cool.

My stud had incredible stamina. We must have been going at it for about thirty minutes. I desperately wanted him to have an incredible orgasm, so I stuck my hand through my legs, past his thrusting cock and down to his large sac. With every stroke, I would lightly squeeze his sensitive balls. That seemed to do it. I glanced back and saw the extreme pleasure in his face. He dug his cock as far as it would go, let out an animal moan and then I felt his come shooting deep inside me. We didn't move until his penis shriveled up and popped out. I could feel his warm come inside my pussy. He pulled my skirt back down over my ass and gave me a tap. I reached back and gave his bulge an approving squeeze. We still hadn't said a word to each other, but then he leaned toward my ear and said I had the best pussy he'd ever fucked. Then he licked my neck.

The concert ended soon after, and everyone slowly went their own way. Mitch grabbed my hand and began pulling me through the thick crowd. A second before I was whisked away, I turned to my stranger and told him he had the best cock I had ever had the pleasure of fucking. And with a quick smile, we parted company. I have never again seen my mystery lover, but you can be sure when I do, there will most certainly be a repeat performance in more intimate surroundings.

Test Flight

As a pilot in the air force, it's one of my jobs to give instructional rides to all the new flyers in our squadron. One cool, March morning I drove to the base, and upon arriving saw that I was scheduled to a check ride with a Lt. Joey Collins. As I got my paperwork together, a stunning redhead, whose sleek five-foot-ten, one-hundred-forty-five-pound frame filled out her flight suit beautifully, came into my office.

"Is this where I'm supposed to sign in for my check flight?" she asked.

"It is," I answered, but not until I looked up and saw that the name tag on her suit read "Collins." I guess the puzzled look on my face was familiar to her. She told me that her last instructor saw the name "Joey" on the sheet and was also expecting a male pilot—until she checked in.

I took her out to the flight line after going over our weather charts and filing our flight plan. After we inspected the plane, we climbed aboard. The crew chief buckled her in her restraint harness and I got strapped into the backseat. We taxied out to the runway. As we rolled out to the centerline, she said over the intercom that this was always the best part of flying for her. I asked her why, but she said she wouldn't be able to tell until we were already up in the air.

Well, I didn't have to wait to know what she was talking about. As soon as she slid the throttles to maximum and lit the afterburner, I instantly knew: The vibrations from the turbines and afterburner sent a raw buzz from my feet to my nose—and I knew she was feeling the same buzz in her crotch!

She finally released the brakes after getting a green light from the tower, and as we took off she let out a long, sexy moan. I felt the stick jerking beneath my hand and realized she was having an orgasm. She confirmed it when she said, "Thanks for the help keeping it straight and level." I told her I wouldn't hold it against her, since I knew she was nervous.

But she calmly replied, "I'm not nervous, sir. I just had a big 'O,' if you know what I mean."

We talked some more as we climbed to altitude. I told her that I once knew another female pilot who had done the same thing on takeoff, and that if she wanted to come in my cockpit it was cool with me.

We completed the flight in about fifteen minutes. After we landed, I told her to report to my office to go over her performance as soon as she took her shower. When she walked in a little while later, I nearly spilled my coffee all over my fresh shirt. She had on a pair of jeans so tight, it looked like she'd been melted into them. Tucked into the narrow waistband was a khaki T-shirt with no bra underneath. She had a great figure and carried herself with the grace of a model.

She smiled and took her seat, first shutting my office door and locking it! I quickly told her I was expecting the base commander, and suggested that it might be better to go over her flight later that evening over dinner. She agreed, and told me to meet her at the end of runway seven at eight o'clock. When she left, chills were coursing through my body.

The whole time the commander was with me, all I could think of was Lt. Collins and how I couldn't wait to take that hot little pilot for a ride of my own. When I got home, there was a message on my recorder from her: "If you're really a jet jock, then have your cock at runway seven by eight o'clock. I'll put it through more moves than an F-16!"

I took a long shower and splashed on some cologne. With a bottle of good champagne tucked under my arm, I slid into the driver's seat of my '67 Corvette. I suddenly realized that the car wouldn't be very comfortable for much necking, let alone fucking or a good 69. But I was confident that we'd find some way to get comfortable.

As I drove past the guard at the gate, she saluted me, and with the top down, I drove off to meet Lt. Collins.

The road I was headed for was off-limits to civilian vehicles, but I told the security police I would be watching some students practice their takeoffs and landings, and they waved me on. I clipped my lights as I pulled to the outer apron of the runway, and sat watching the sunset while listening to some classic Zombies on the tape deck.

I saw a car coming. My cock got hard just from the thought of what was in store for me. As Collins pulled up in her red Miata, I got out of my 'Vette and told her that we might have a problem, since neither of our cars was big enough for much activity.

"No sweat," she said, and quickly pulled a sleeping bag and a couple of blankets from her car!

She stepped up to me and I pulled her close, sucking her tongue deep into my mouth. While we kissed, I opened my eyes to see her already writhing with lust. We spread the blankets and sleeping bag open, and soon we were both stark naked. I slipped my mouth down to her tummy and had started licking my way cuntward, when I realized she had shaved her pussy. It felt so good to rub the smooth skin while feasting on her clit, which was sticking way out. I hummed "The Star Spangled Banner" as she put my head in a massive leg lock and commanded me to keep sucking!

After she came several times, she finally released her hold on me. "Get ready to have your cock sucked," she said. "I mean *really* sucked."

And suck she did! Her throat must have been bottomless. She was rocking up and down on me like an oil rig, when all of a sudden I noticed a set of lights coming toward us. I was so close to the edge, though, that I didn't say a word until I felt the last of my hot come blast down her throat.

Then we both heard a car door slam. Lt. Collins jerked her head up and gasped. Since we were both officers, I knew I could take care of whoever was checking up on us. Still, it could prove to be an embarrassing situation. But as it turned out, it was the pretty, young security officer from the front gate who'd waved me through earlier. She beamed her flashlight on us just as we were diving under the blankets.

She started to ask if everything was okay, when she suddenly giggled and said, "Joey?"

"Is that you, Anita?" Joey stammered. It seems they were roommates in an off-base apartment. Anita walked back to her car and got on the radio, then came back and told us that she was "officially" on her dinner break. She and Joey talked for a minute while I walked back to my car to get the champagne. When I got back, Anita was taking her shirt off and Joey asked me if it was all right if Anita joined us. I didn't even bother answering. All I did was grab them both and pull them down to the blanket with me.

They took turns sucking my prick, and then ate each other out. With a little persuasion, I got Anita to sit on my cock and ride it while Joey rode my face with her pretty, shaved cunt. I shot my load up Anita's tight box just as Joey flooded my mouth with her tangy juices. All the while we were doing this, there were planes taking off and landing not fifty feet away from us, roaring their engines and shooting flames out of their exhaust. It seemed that each time a plane took off, my cock was ready for another go with one of these two fine ladies.

Anita told Joey she wished she knew someone who could take her for a ride in one of those planes. Joey replied, "You do now!" She told her that I was a pilot and a flight instructor and that I'd be more than happy to take her up. Without hesitation, I agreed to do just that.

Now that I'm not stationed on that base anymore, I often think back to that night on runway seven. Shortly thereafter, I took Anita for that plane ride. (We ended up fucking before we even took off!) The three of us spent many happy weekends together that summer.

By the way, Joey and I got married last year, and yes, we still enjoy flying!

Ride 'Em

I bought a horse on a whim, and then found out I couldn't ride him. He was an ex-racing thoroughbred named Miracle, and he would ride away with me. Either I found a good trainer, or I'd have to sell him. I decided to try the trainer route first.

Her name was Trish, and the people at the stable where I boarded my horse told me that she was the best trainer around. She was petite, with curly red hair and a tight little ass. When I first saw her she was wearing a pair of tight, white britches and tall, black riding boots. I introduced myself and explained my problem, and she agreed to look at my horse.

Trish was impressed by Miracle's size and asked if she could ride him. "Fine," I said, and helped her tack him up. She was very businesslike. I, on the other hand, couldn't help but notice her tasty ass and the way her pert breasts pressed against her shirt. She popped right on top of him with no assistance. Trish was muscular but still very feminine, and I was strongly attracted to her. I envied Miracle as she mounted him effortlessly. I wished it was me she was about to ride.

My horse put Trish to the test, taking the turns fast and

bucking erratically. But she countered his every attempt to throw her, and pretty soon had mastered the beast. After about forty-five more minutes of riding his graceful form, she got off and said, "He needs to learn some manners, but he really can move." I asked if she would train us together. She agreed and we set up a lesson, adding that this session was a freebie. But I insisted on doing something, so she let me buy her dinner.

That evening, her transformation from stable hand to elegant woman was spectacular! Her shimmering red hair lay in ringlets around her shoulders. I looked closely, for the first time, at her green eyes and high cheekbones. She was wearing a silky, black dress that was gathered with a clasp at her breasts. High heels and black stockings completed the outfit.

Trish was quiet and shy as we drove to dinner—quite a difference from the woman who had so handily tamed Miracle a few hours earlier. I found the contrast appealing indeed. The meal was delicious, and although we made small talk as we ate, by the time we'd finished our second bottle of wine all I could think about was how hot I was to make love to her. Remembering how well she had handled herself in the saddle, I knew she'd be a spirited partner in the sack. Hopeful that we'd have a long and rewarding night together, I ordered dessert.

We shared a great big wedge of cheesecake dripping with strawberries. I offered her a piece on my fork. Taking my hand in hers, she slid the cake into her mouth and slowly withdrew the empty fork. A bit of strawberry juice lingered on her lips. It was making me very horny and she knew it too. As I moved to remove the juice with my napkin, she deftly caught it with the tip of her tongue. She smiled coyly and giggled at my growing discomfort. I shifted nervously in my seat.

"Now it's my turn to feed you," she said. Taking the

fork, she offered me some cake. As I took it in my mouth, she let out a muffled sigh of pleasure. This really unnerved me, and I blushed. She giggled again, and this time I laughed back.

We really began to enjoy each other's company. As I offered her piece after piece of cake, I felt a nudge on the inside of my calf. She was working her toe up my pants leg. I almost dropped the fork as I watched her tease another piece of cake into her sensuous mouth. We laughed at our flirtations and moved closer together, feeding off of each other's desire.

As she leaned toward me, I got a good look at her nipples, erect and straining under her dress. I moved my hand to her leg and gave it a gentle squeeze. She looked approvingly in my eyes and opened her legs slightly. I moved my hand to her inner thigh and began to stroke her leg. She squeezed her legs together and moaned with pleasure at my touch. Her fragrance began to intoxicate me. Our heads moved closer together—but just as we were about to kiss, the waiter approached the table with the check. Trish began to laugh. I asked her if she was ready, and she replied, "For the last half an hour, at least."

Before we got in the car, I pulled her to me and kissed her passionately. It was as if a floodgate had opened and released our pent-up passions. Hungrily we explored each other's mouth as our fingers searched out the sensitive parts of our bodies. Realizing that this was not the place to consummate our passion, we got in the car.

As I drove, I told her I wanted to make love to her. "Yes," she answered, putting her hand on my thigh, "so do I. But first we must stop off at the stable. I need to check on a horse. He pulled a tendon earlier today and I want to see if the swelling is down." She moved her hand over my growing bulge. "I just hope it's not as swelled as this is right now," she said of my throbbing member.

I was embarrassed by her brazenness. Trish apparently enjoyed sex as much as I did and was not afraid to show it. I'd never had the good luck to be with such a woman, and I was ready to enjoy every moment.

The stable was dark and quiet. Taking Trish by the hand, I kissed her again. Laughing, she pulled her head back and said, "I bet you've never made love in the hay before." Well, she was right. Before I could say anything, though, she pushed me away and ran, giggling, into the barn, tossing her shoes off behind her. I followed in hot pursuit. When I found her she was hiding behind a door. I picked her up and carried her to an empty stall that had been cleaned out. On the way, she snatched up a blanket. I put her down and she covered the ground with the blanket. Kissing hard, we eased ourselves down. The only sound, other than our pounding hearts, was the stirring of the sleeping horses.

I slowly ran a hand under her skirt. As I ran my hand along the inside of her creamy thigh, I realized she wasn't wearing any panties. I began to squeeze and explore. She unbuttoned my shirt, then sucked and bit my nipples. Our hips gyrated in unison. With my free hand I unfastened her dress and peeled it away, as if pulling petals off a rose.

Trish had a beautifully toned body. Her breasts were petite but firm, the nipples erect and proud. Her pussy was framed by closely trimmed wisps of red hair, and glistened in the moonlight streaming in through the stable door. I removed my shirt and our bodies met, their warmth insulating us from the cool night. We kissed and fondled each other with unbridled passion. The horses began to stir as our moans grew louder.

She rolled me onto my back and unbuckled my pants. Sliding her hands inside my briefs, she pumped my throbbing prick. In an instant she had stripped me naked and was rubbing the head of my cock between her fingers. When I tried to suck her nipples into my mouth, she pushed me away and said, "Just relax. We have all night." Starting at the center of my chest, she traced a wet path with her tongue down to my stiff cock and guided it into her waiting mouth. With her tongue she tickled the head and shaft. Slowly, she worked my engorged cock into her hot, hungry mouth. The pleasure was intense. I was completely at her mercy!

I ran my fingers through her hair and caressed her body. It felt so good I didn't want it to end. I felt a familiar rumble in my balls that told me I was close to climaxing. I told her this, but she wouldn't let up. All she said was, "Relax and enjoy it." I ran my fingers through her hair as I climaxed. With half a dozen spasms of pleasure I came in her mouth. She continued sucking and swallowing until the last drop was gone.

Getting up, our strength slowly came back. I took her in my arms and said, "Now it's my turn." I kissed her, tracing circles around her lips, ears and nipples with my tongue. Sliding my hand between her thighs, I stroked and squeezed them gently. Her moans told me I was on the right track. I ran my fingers through her pubic hair and searched out her pussy. It was moist and responsive. She squirmed under my caresses. I worked my finger in and out until she was dripping with pleasure.

After sucking each breast in turn, I drew a wet path with my tongue to her waiting pussy. Gently spreading her lips, I found her clitoris with the tip of my tongue. I maintained pressure on her breasts by pinching her nipples between my fingers. She gyrated, bucked uncontrollably and begged me to increase the tempo. I did so, and she responded with a shriek of pleasure that echoed through the quiet of the stable.

"Boy," she said when she'd caught her breath, "I sure needed that."

It wasn't long before we were ready for another round.

This time I slid on top of her and rubbed my hard cock between her legs. She wrapped her fingers around it and whispered, "So what do you plan to do with this?" In answer, I slipped my rod past her velvety cunt lips with one quick stroke.

She kept her fingers wrapped around the base of my prick as I worked it in and out of her grotto. She was tight but wet. As our passion grew, so did our rhythm. She whispered in my ear, "I love to feel you fuck me. Do it hard." I pumped with all of my might and we soon exploded in mutual ecstasy. Our bodies covered with sweat, we lay in the dark, completely satisfied.

Eventually we got up and picked the straw from each other's hair and body. We got dressed and looked over her horse. He was doing fine. Then we returned to Trish's place, showered, and enjoyed a restful sleep. In the morning we were refreshed and started the day off by making love. I guess I lucked out. Not only did I find an excellent horse trainer, but I got a great lover in the bargain.

Wives on the Waves

It began innocently enough. I was working through my vacation as first mate on a forty-foot cabin cruiser in the Caribbean. The captain, my friend, was kind enough to keep me employed all of my summers through college. As a charter, we usually had from four to six people aboard for short cruises. Generally our passengers were middle-aged businessmen and their wives or girlfriends. On one particular cruise I really lucked out, having two young couples on board for an extended weekend. I certainly didn't expect any sex, but it was nice to see two beautiful women sunning themselves on the deck, even if their husbands were also on the boat. While serving brunch to the two ladies our first morning out, one of them kept staring at me—and at my bathing trunks. This struck me as odd, considering she had an attractive husband below who was, presumably, sleeping. I might as well interject here that I am five feet nine inches tall, and have brown hair and brown eyes. I am in good shape, although I'll admit I'm certainly no Adonis.

When they finished eating, the women asked me to sit with them for a bit. Henry, the captain, was managing the ship, so I felt comfortable relaxing for a few minutes. They introduced themselves as Christine and Nancy. I told them my name and we exchanged pleasantries. I finally got up enough nerve to ask where their husbands were. Christine leaned forward to speak, and in doing so her towel fell off her shoulders, expressing a pair of incredibly full breasts. She blushed and put the towel back in place, although I must say she didn't seem in any big hurry to do so.

Christine and Nancy told me that their husbands were bisexual and, as Nancy put it, "hot for each other." Both wives were willing to let the men have their little getaways, like this one, as long as they didn't go off to find any other men. As part of the deal, the trysts always took place in an exotic setting, and the women always got to come along for the ride. And this, they explained, was one of those rides.

The two beauties went on to say that while they didn't mind getting it on in a group, straight girl-on-girl action didn't excite them much. I pointedly asked if they wanted to party with Henry and me, and was pleased (even a little shocked) to hear them both say yes.

I excused myself and went to tell Henry the good news. He smiled but, brandishing his wedding band with a sigh, told me I was on my own. "Knock yourself out," he said with envy dripping from his voice, adding that I could use the crew's quarters in the bow of the boat.

I ran back to the ladies, escorted them down to the cabin and carefully locked the door behind me. I got out some tequila and poured three generous shots. We continued to get acquainted, with lots of physical contact between the shots of tequila. Soon Nancy and Christine had my trunks off. Their hands and mouths were all over my body. It was a dream come true.

Those two sumptuous, raven-haired women did things to my cock I still think about to this day. Nancy positioned herself between my legs and gave my balls a tongue bath, while Christine offered the same treatment to my cock. Christine, in particular, had an incredible mouth. Her tongue never seemed to stop moving. It felt as though my prick was being given a nonstop massage. Looking down, I was so turned on I almost passed out.

I asked Nancy to remove her bathing suit and have a seat. She laughed and asked me where. I flicked my tongue in response, and soon she was astride my face, her thick, pink love lips parting for my tongue. The exotic smell of her cunt filled my nostrils. I had never been so happy in all my life. The sensations, tastes and smells were driving me insane with lust. My tongue and lips danced over Nancy's pussy so quickly and with so much intensity that for a minute I didn't notice what had happened: Christine had taken a seat as well—right on my throbbing cock!

It didn't seem as though any of us would ever tire out, so intense was the fucking and tonguing taking place in that little cabin. I'm proud to admit that I always last a good, long while in bed. I can exercise excellent control over my orgasms, which guarantees that my partners and I always get our fill. When I finally do come, though, I'm like a wild animal. And I knew that time was approaching.

Nancy was really getting into riding my face, and Christine was slowly easing her way up and down my cock. With one hand rubbing her clit and the other stroking my balls, she looked incredible. Her hair was tossed back. A dew of sweat covered her smooth body. Her eyes were glazed over and her tight stomach was heaving in what I knew was the beginning of an orgasm. She looked more sensational than any actress I'd ever seen in an erotic video. But what made this picture perfect was the frame: I was watching the whole fantastic scene through the gap between Nancy's luscious thighs!

Soon Christine was bucking frantically, grinding herself all the way down against the base of my shaft. She came, and I felt her juices massaging my cock as they dripped out of her satisfied pussy. I felt an incredible sensation beginning in my stomach and spreading through my entire body. I swear, I blacked out for a split second when I came. But come I did, blasting jets of hot sperm into Christine's cunt.

Nancy collapsed by my side on the bed, and I quickly lifted her leg and began feasting on her again from a different angle. I was happy to feel Christine's lips again at work on my prick. The best surprise, however, was glancing up to see Nancy eating Christine's sopping-wet pussy. What a turn-on! I couldn't help myself and emptied another load into Christine's mouth.

After a while we all collapsed in a heap on the bed. The smell of sex threatened to overpower the tiny cabin. I opened a porthole to let in the cool sea air, thinking of poor, married Henry upstairs in his captain's chair.

Soon Christine suggested a shower and a swim. The shower turned into another suck-and-fuck fest almost as intense as the first, but nothing will ever equal that first time with those two special women. I shake my head sadly when I think of what their husbands missed out on.

Heart & Soul

A few years ago I tended bar in a soul club that catered to a mostly black clientele. I was the only white person that worked there, although, since I have a shaved head and a dark, rich tan, people often mistook me for black in the club's dim light.

The minute Anita walked into the room I knew she was special. She carried herself like royalty and her clothes and jewelry spelled class. She was super fine, and she knew it.

There was chemistry between us from the start. We spent the entire evening talking. I couldn't let her get away without asking for a date, and with a dazzling smile and a soft laugh she said, "Yes."

When the day of our date finally arrived I picked Anita up at her home. After I met her family we left for the restaurant. But something was wrong. She seemed stiff and uncomfortable. She sat against the door with her hand on the handle.

Suddenly it dawned on me. "You didn't realize I was white, did you?"

There was a quiet "No." Her eyes never left the road ahead.

I asked her if she wanted me to take her home. Again her answer was "No."

Anita never totally relaxed the entire evening, but from this awkward beginning came a long and eventually beautiful friendship.

Anita was proud of her ethnic heritage. As a Black Muslim she was extremely angry about the way the white power structure treated her people. Our discussions on the subject were often heated.

One night she said, "Greg, you know we don't often tell people, and we are not too proud of it, but I've got a grandmother who is part white."

After a few minutes of silence I responded, "What would you say, Anita, if I told you that we don't often tell people and we are not too proud of it, but I've got a grandmother who is part black?"

For a while she just looked at the floor. Then she murmured, "I didn't say that, did I?" For all she taught me, I was able to show her that the very thing she hated most—prejudice—was lurking in her own heart.

James Baldwin once wrote that white men lust after black women because they want to be the "master," to subjugate and violate them. I am not sure where Mr. Baldwin got his information, but he sure wasn't talking about Anita and me. She made it rough on me. She kept making rules, erecting barriers as if she wanted me to become discouraged and quit. Many times I almost got to the point where I was ready to give up on her, but something about Anita kept me coming back.

After several dates Anita began to notice my frequent use of slightly risqué humor. "Sex is a big thing with you, isn't it?" she asked. I admitted that I thought it was an important part of a male/female relationship, something of great beauty when shared.

She nodded and said, "Okay, next Thursday." It was as if she had just made up her mind to have the car lubed. I protested that it was not necessary, preferring no sex at all to a cold, passionless "service job." But she had made up her mind, and nothing I said would make any difference.

Thursday came and we decided to take a brief out-of-town trip. Anita didn't want anyone in our community to even think we were lovers, much less catch us going into a motel. Unfortunately there was a convention in town, and after being turned away from several motels we headed home. I thought I heard a small sigh of relief. As we passed a Holiday Inn we decided to try one last time.

When I returned to the car, she looked up with a faint smile and said, "No luck, huh?" When I dangled the room keys, she shrank back into the seat, her smile gone. I felt an odd mixture of irritation and amusement. It was obvious the last thing Anita wanted was to hop into bed with a white man.

After we found our room Anita rushed to take a shower. I smiled again as I heard her lock the bathroom door. When she emerged, in a cloud of steam, she was wrapped head to toe in towels. She imperiously announced that I could now use the shower.

I half expected her to be gone when I came out, but she was watching television with the blankets tight around her chin. The mound of towels on the floor indicated she was naked beneath the covers. I sat down on the edge of the bed and we both pretended to watch the show.

Without saying a word, I turned and looked at her. She said, "Don't rush me." I smiled and pretended to watch TV again.

After a few minutes I leaned over and kissed her. Not our usual goodnight peck, but a moist, sweet kiss. All the walls came tumbling down. No black, no white, just a man and a woman. As I slid beneath the covers our naked bodies melted together.

I pulled back. I had dreamed of this moment for so long. Slowly I gazed at her nakedness. She was an ebony Venus, exquisite in every detail. Each beautiful breast was full and round, with a dark, swollen nipple that looked like a ripe blackberry. Between her satin-smooth thighs was a glistening wedge of dark curls. When I finally looked up there was a smile on her lips.

As I began kissing and licking her inner thighs, she leaned back and opened up to me. Her pussy was like a beautiful exotic flower. Each petal was trimmed in ebony while the center was a rich pink. As my tongue caressed her, sweet nectar flowed to my lips. Her hands urged me on. As I licked her clit, spasms shook her body. She began to moan and arch to meet my hungry mouth.

I moved up until I was looking into her half-closed, lust-filled eyes. The head of my swollen cock pressed against her hot, moist cunt. Slowly I slid into her. With each inch, her eyes grew wider. At first I took my time. Each stroke was long, slow and deep. She felt so good. Her pussy was tight, holding my dick like an old friend.

As our passion grew, our speed increased. Breathing became shallow and rapid. Sweat poured from our bodies.

Anita cried out, "Oh yes, oh yes! Fuck me baby, fuck me!" I was only too happy to obey. I felt the pleasure building. I tried to hold back, but there was no stopping. Grabbing her beautiful ass, I buried my rod deep inside her. My cock erupted, pulsing with each spurt. She wrapped her arms around me with a moan, and I felt her body shudder.

Now when someone mentions race relations I can't help but smile a little. I've learned a lot about the subject from Anita, and I like to think I've taught her a thing or two in return.

Office Orientation

Our receptionist is an eighteen-year-old girl who is the epitome of innocence. She looks almost like a librarian, but a very sexy librarian.

I saw in her eyes a thirst for life and its challenges. As the human resources manager for a large Midwest company, it was my job to give direction and nourishment to her desires. Since she was new to the corporate world, I decided I would really take her under my wing.

Her name is Debbie. She has a great body, but the clothes she chose to wear seemed like attempts to hide it. During the course of our many conversations I discovered the reason. She was very shy, having lived a relatively sheltered life in a small, rural community. I realized she needed more than simply company orientation. She needed orientation to life.

We made plans to spend a weekend together. I wanted to take her shopping—let her know what it is like to "go out with the girls." When the weekend arrived I picked her up at her apartment and we headed for the mall. I told Debbie that we would find clothes that were a bit more stylish than what she was accustomed to wearing. She excitedly agreed.

We stopped at a large department store and proceeded to

the ladies' department. I picked out a few sensuous outfits for her, and we both went into the dressing room. Debbie tried them on. As she was changing I caught my first glimpse of what she really looks like—a beautiful young woman, fully developed in every sense of the phrase. Until then I had not paid much attention to her body because it had been so disguised. She had the figure of a goddess. Her breasts were firm and uplifted, with nipples that seemed to point at me. Her cunt had sparse blonde hair that revealed much of her pussy. I felt it was a sin for her to not show off her fine attributes.

I was feeling familiar stirrings within me as I watched Debbie try on the different outfits. I had never felt that way toward a member of my own sex. I felt confused: contradicting thoughts were fluttering through my mind.

I decided we were going to spice up her outfits a bit more than I had planned. I took her to the lingerie department.

I picked out some garter belts, bras, panties, teddies and a few other accessories which, I explained to her, would help her feel good about herself. I told her I usually wear them myself because they are so comfortable. Debbie was skeptical at first, but decided to go along because I was being so nice to spend time with her.

After I picked out some items, we headed back to the dressing room. She fumbled with the garter belt, so I helped her attach it to the stockings, accidentally touching her thighs in the process. I wanted to grab her, yet I was afraid of how she might react.

I am not sure who shuddered more when she pulled the G-string up her long thighs and, innocently enough, pulled too far, sliding the silky material into her cunt. I enjoyed watching her as she slid a finger in to retrieve the G-string from her warm, moist depths. I could tell she was as excited as I was.

Next I helped her put on a skimpy little bra I had picked out. I enjoyed the softness of her breasts, and I spent a little extra time making sure the fit was good. Her nipples were hard and erect, pointing out at me in an inviting way. We looked deep into each other's eyes as I finished her fitting. I was about to tell her we should be going, when she raised her finger to my lips to silence me. I gently began licking and sucking her finger. Surprise and lust were written on her face as I moved from her finger to her nipples, then down to taste another woman's pussy for the first time in my life.

Debbie lay back on the little stool. I was on fire as I pulled the G-string to one side and slid a finger into her honey-pot. I lowered my mouth and drove my tongue into her as far as I could, savoring her sweet taste. She came instantly, with a loud moan that brought a salesclerk running in to see what was the matter.

"Is everything all right in there?" she asked.

We both started giggling. "Everything is dandy," I answered.

We heard the salesclerk leave. I gave Debbie a soft kiss on the lips, gently sliding my tongue into her mouth. I held her breasts in my hands and felt the soft firmness. I caressed her nipples and she arched her back, moaning in delight, wrapping her arms around me and pulling me toward her so that our tummies and breasts touched. I was aware of a growing wetness between my legs, and wanted nothing more than to have her press her hot, young mouth against me and suck my sweet nectar like there was no tomorrow.

We quickly got dressed and walked out of the dressing room. Since the G-string was soaked from her arousal, I put it back on the shelf and grabbed another one. The salesclerk who had heard us in the dressing room gave me a sly look and smiled. I smiled back, starting to again feel hot stirrings between my legs. Having sex with another woman was having a bigger impact on me than I thought it would. I was becoming insatiable for my own sex!

We quickly paid for the merchandise and hurried to make the appointment with the hairdresser.

After we reached the salon I instructed Jackie, the hairdresser, to give Debbie a more contemporary look. I sat down to watch.

I watched Jackie and admired the firm flare of her hips and her shapely breasts. For the third time that day I started getting hot over a woman. Debbie noticed me staring at the stylist, and I think she felt somewhat jealous. As I sized Jackie up, Debbie began slowly spreading her legs under the bib so that I could see right up to her cunt. The G-string slid into her pussy. Her legs were encased in white lace stockings held up by the garter belt. Debbie lifted her knees slightly to give me a better view.

I was having a difficult time maintaining a conversation with Jackie. I think she knew that I was staring up Debbie's dress. Then Debbie began tracing the line of the G-string with her middle finger. Seeing this, I moaned. By this time Jackie was fully aware of what was going on. She said after she finished Debbie's hair she would be glad to "help me out," if I cared to wait around until lunchtime. I told her, with a chuckle, that I didn't think I could last that long.

Upon hearing that, Jackie locked the door and drew the shades. I was glad that we were lucky enough to be the only people in the salon. Jackie removed her clothes and insisted that Debbie and I undress as well. Debbie sat back and enjoyed orgasm after orgasm as Jackie and I licked her all over, nibbling on her most sensitive places. Then Jackie climbed up on the chair and sat on Debbie's lap, facing her, letting her breasts dangle in front of Debbie's mouth. She hungrily lapped and fondled Jackie's breasts.

I had a feast before me—two wet cunts staring me in the

face. My tongue and fingers brought them both to orgasm, and they collapsed together.

I started to finger my own cunt while waiting for Jackie to quickly finish Debbie's perm. I was so wet I began smearing the juice all over Debbie's lips, giving her a taste of my pussy.

Finally it was done. Debbie looked incredible. The farm girl had been transformed into a woman of the 1990s. We quickly grabbed our clothes, put on just enough to cover ourselves and headed for Jackie's place, where we would be more comfortable.

As Jackie drove, I went down on Debbie again, bringing her to more orgasms. I loved the way she cried out when I ran my tongue along her hot clit. God, she could buck and bounce.

"I want to eat you," she told me. I had no problem with that. I lay down on the backseat and she got down between my legs. I was in heaven as she slowly ran her tongue along the soft folds of my pussy. When she wrapped her lips around my clit, my ass shot up off the seat and I was crying out, so loud I surprised myself. I came and my juice dribbled out of my pussy. Debbie licked it up. Smiling, she said, "Good to the last drop."

"You know, you two are driving me crazy," Jackie said. She was doing all she could to drive with one hand while manipulating her cunt with the other. Debbie and I reached over the seat and began fondling Jackie's tits as she drove.

Jackie's apartment is on the first floor, and she has underground parking. After parking the car we ran into her apartment and picked up where we left off. We didn't even make it to her bedroom for a couple of hours. The living room floor was fine with us.

We were three sex-starved ladies with a wealth of sexual

energy at our disposal. We tried everything possible. Jackie had the most experience with woman-to-woman sex because many of her customers come on to her. It seems many of them get excited during the long hairstyling sessions, in which Jackie innocently rubs her body against them while doing her work. Jackie has made a lot of money taking special care of her "regulars."

Being intimately involved with some customers has enabled her to perfect the fine art of shaving and sculpting pubic hair. She had a photo album full of pictures of her work. Debbie and I got horny all over again after we looked through it.

Jackie taught Debbie and I plenty about the art of making love. She had a huge trunk of goodies—sex toys—that brought us to new heights of delight. We used every device at least once. We enjoyed what we did with the two-headed dildo the best.

After going at it for hours, we all fell asleep together. When we awoke a short time later we raided the refrigerator. We had built up hearty appetites, and knew we would need the strength for our next session.

At work Debbie and I keep our distance, which is often difficult. Debbie occasionally takes days off when I am out recruiting at colleges. She accompanies me as a representative. I have her dress very businesslike, but only on the outside. If her jacket were to be opened, anyone watching would be in for a surprise. I always get wet just thinking of how little she has on underneath.

Debbie's ability to charm has been instrumental in helping me hire a number of male and female coeds. Once, during a lengthy recruiting trip, we had not found time for loving. It was late in the afternoon and we still had one more interview—and on top of that, a long drive ahead of us. We were more than a little bit grouchy when the last girl showed up. You can imagine how delighted we were to discover how beautiful she was.

The room was arranged so that Colleen the candidate and I were facing each other. Debbie sat next to Colleen.

Debbie fidgeted in her chair as she began the opening remarks and basic questioning. I watched to see how well the candidate handled herself. When I caught Debbie's glance I licked my lips and looked at our candidate, Colleen. Debbie knew right away what to do. She spread her legs just enough to allow me a view of her panty-clad crotch.

Debbie then adjusted her suit jacket so her breasts were visible. Her nipples stretched against the silk blouse. Colleen continued to answer our questions. Debbie then arranged her chair so that she was facing Colleen, giving her the same tantalizing view of her pussy I had. Colleen became nervous and struggled to keep her attention from Debbie's crotch. The more Debbie fidgeted, the more her skirt slid up her thighs, exposing the tops of her stockings.

Colleen tried to avoid looking at Debbie by turning toward me. I picked up the conversation. This gave Debbie, a true exhibitionist, the chance to open her blouse, exposing a half-bra that uplifted her perky breasts. Debbie deftly removed her jacket and blouse, and then unhooked her skirt, letting it fall. She was standing behind Colleen wearing only her bra, G-string, garter belt and stockings. She began masturbating. I tried to pay attention to the candidate. Colleen, meanwhile, could not help but hear Debbie's activity. Nevertheless, she refused to turn around. Her face was flushed and she was breathing hard.

I said there was one more question I wanted to ask her. I watched a look of relief come over her pretty face.

I asked Colleen if she was interested in learning more intimate aspects of corporate culture. She stared at me silently for the longest time. I could imagine the thoughts going through her head. They were probably similar to those I had had while in the dressing room with Debbie.

She blurted out, "Yes."

I instructed her to turn around. I wondered what her reaction would be after she saw Debbie standing there with a finger in her clean-shaven cunt.

Colleen gasped. I began caressing her from behind as Debbie's fingers quickened their thrusts into her cunt. I took Colleen's suit jacket off. She didn't resist in the slightest, and merely continued watching Debbie and licking her lips. Next I unbuttoned her blouse and skirt and removed them. I kept caressing her as I undressed her.

Debbie then approached Colleen and hugged her. Colleen still had not said a word. Debbie pulled Colleen's hips against her own, and they ground their cunts together.

Colleen was beginning to loosen up. She let out little sighs and ran her hands all over Debbie. I was not going to be left out. I quickly took my clothes off, reached between their legs and started fingering and licking their cunts. Colleen's was tight and juicy, and she tasted marvelous. It took only moments to bring her to orgasm.

Debbie gently pushed Colleen onto her knees in front of her. With one hand, Debbie pulled her G-string aside and with the other she pulled Colleen's face into her cunt. Colleen's nervous inexperience was quickly replaced with energetic enthusiasm. Her tongue quickly brought Debbie off.

We had to get out of the interview room before the placement-office staff became suspicious. We put on only our suits, stuffing our underwear in our purses, and quickly left to go to Colleen's apartment. The ride there was enjoyable, as we continued petting in the car. Colleen had adapted so well to our advances, I couldn't help feeling impressed.

Colleen led us to her bedroom and we all undressed. We

began an intense fucking session. It wasn't long before Maria, Colleen's roommate, walked in on us. We were not about to let her run away. Maria nervously resisted our advances, but gave in shortly after Colleen's tongue darted into her pussy. Then I placed my cunt over Maria's mouth, and Debbie caressed the girl's body. We managed to bring her to one sweet orgasm after another, within seconds.

Debbie and I were quite satisfied when we left Colleen's, and eagerly delighted that Colleen and Maria had joined our group.

Strip Trip

I'm just an average girl. When I walk down the street, men don't turn around to look at me. But an experience I had recently proved to me that anything can happen, especially if you take the initiative.

One of my good friends was getting married, so a few of us took her out to an all-male revue. We made sure that we were sitting at tables in the front row so we could stuff bills under the guys' G-strings and slide our hands inside their bikinis.

Once the show started, all I could think about was what it would be like to actually have sex with one of these men. Judging from the way they moved their bodies, I figured that any one of them would be great in bed. They all looked like they knew how to hit the right spot, how to push a girl over the edge of ecstasy. I had a plan that might work, but knowing my luck, I thought it would turn out to be just another fantasy I could think about while I used my trusty vibrator.

I went to the ladies' room and took out five one-dollar bills. Then I took a red pen and wrote a message on the edge of all the bills. It said: "Hi! Would you like to have a party with a very horny lady? If so, come to Susie's at nine-thirty tomorrow night." Then I wrote my address and added, "I'll be waiting." I returned to our table and set my plan in motion. The next five studs who danced within my reach got a bill with my message on it.

The following morning I got my hair done and had a facial. I bought three different kinds of wine, and I bought the sexiest and sleaziest outfit I could find. It was made out of black lace and nothing else.

When I got home I dressed, drank some wine and waited. I sat and watched the clock, second after second, minute after minute, hour after hour. When it was only five after eight, I heard a knock on the door. Great, I thought, here's somebody I'll have to get rid of fast.

I answered the door and my heart stopped. Standing in the hall was not one, but three of the male strippers from the night before. I couldn't believe it. Here I was, standing with three incredibly gorgeous guys. I just froze and didn't say anything.

One of them asked if I was Susie. I replied, "Yes. Come in, please."

The guy who had asked my name told me that he was Dave, and introduced the others, Jeff and Brad. Dave went on to say that they were sorry they'd showed up early but it would give us all more time to get to know each other. I offered them each a glass of wine.

Before we knew it, one glass led to another, and before long we were all very relaxed and talking as if we all had known each other for some time. I was feeling very fine and I confessed to them that I was very turned on by their performances at the club.

Jeff stood up and said, "Well, we'll perform for you right now." Brad tuned the stereo to a different station and began to dance around. I was getting very hot. Jeff pulled me up to him. I took over from there. I grabbed Jeff, pulled his body close to me and kissed him. As I was kissing him, I felt the other two strippers' hands on my body. One was working on my shirt buttons and the other on my skirt zipper. Things started going the way I'd hoped.

I had only wanted one of them but I sure wasn't going to turn the others away. I'd thought about having two men at once, but three? I felt like I was the luckiest woman on earth. I was naked and wondering what was going to happen next. Then Don lowered me onto the couch and plunged his thick cock into my pussy.

I was in heaven. Don was fucking me with long strokes, slow and easy. Jeff and Brad each had one tit in their mouths. I never thought I would enjoy having an audience. But to be truthful, the thought of all three of them watching me turned me on even more. When Don shot his load inside me, Brad and Jeff both kept sucking my tits.

I wanted more. I stood up, pushed Jeff to the floor and jumped upon his hard tool. I was riding him when I felt a pair of lips close over one of my breasts and suck my nipple. That got me thinking. I wondered what it would be like to have one cock in my pussy and one in my mouth at the same time. Brad was sucking my tit, so I reached for Don's cock and pulled him to my mouth. As I sucked Don's cock, I reached down and started stroking Brad's cock.

We carried on like this for at least another hour. I was fucked by each of them and sucked by each of them. And you know what? I was right. They *did* know just the moves that could push a woman over the brink. I never came so many times in my life, even counting marathon sessions with my vibrator. By the time we all fell asleep on the floor, I don't think there were any positions we hadn't been in.

When I woke up at dawn, my three studs were gone. But

they'd left something behind. Next to a bottle of wine, I found three dollar bills. Each of my studs had left one with his name, phone number, and address written on it in red ink, and an invitation to call any time.

I haven't decided what to do yet. Maybe I'll call one of them. On the other hand, I've got plenty of one-dollar bills.

French Girl

I'm married, forty, with two kids. My wife and I are happy. But we haven't had sex since our second was born three years ago. I love my wife, need her, and wouldn't leave her. Yet our lack of a sex life together made the episodes I'm about to relate all the more intense.

Last summer we were visited by Annette, a nineteen-year-old daughter of good friends. She's from Paris. She was touring the States, hiking and sightseeing, and stayed with us for a week. Annette was pleasant and friendly. Her English wasn't perfect, but it was fairly good. She baby-sat our kids a couple of nights so we could go out. After that week, she planned to hike from a trail near our home, meeting up with other French students at a hostel some miles to the north.

Let me tell you about Annette. She's five foot two, a bundle of energy with short, chestnut hair. She has deep green eyes, a thin, hourglass shape, and never wears makeup. Her breasts are small but very firm, with scarlet brown nipples. Her pubic hair is elongated and wispy. She's not at all like the women portrayed in explicit movies. In comparison to her, they're cold platinum. Annette has freckles over her back, arms and legs, and a slightly oversize nose. She's real.

I saw her, considered her youth, appetite, comeliness, and had the natural thoughts. I also felt the natural inhibitions. Besides the mixed emotions, there wasn't opportunity. But early one afternoon, my wife took the kids to a party at a friend's house. She was only supposed to be gone for ninety minutes. I watched over a cooking roast, its hearty odors making Annette and me hungry. We read. She sat in a chair across the room. I admit I was watching her as well, trembling and growing hard. I finally broke through my indecision, got up and pulled a chair up beside her. We talked about her day, her visit. We talked about small things, anything.

I went around the back of her chair and started rubbing her shoulders. She didn't ask me to. She didn't object or encourage. She sat there silently. I slid up the midlength sleeves of a Madras shirt, stroking her upper arms, her lower arms, caressing her hands, her fingers. I asked, "Do you mind?" She said at once, "No," and shook her head slightly, her hair bouncing as she did. "It feels good," she admitted. My heart leapt.

I moved around in front of her, sitting on the floor between her crossed legs, bare from the thighs, revealed by khaki shorts. I touched her legs, to and fro, above her knees, inside her thighs. I caressed them, and bent over and kissed them, lightly, gently. She spread her legs, and I gave them the same gentle, loving attentions.

Suddenly, we heard the garage door opening. I quickly moved to the other side of the room. I said to Annette, "Sorry." She looked at me with disappointed eyes, and nodded. The most difficult thing to mask was my very hard cock, and perhaps, our mutual nervousness. I don't think my wife noticed, and it subsided. No other opportunities presented themselves that week.

Annette left us early the following Sunday, giving us

friendly hugs and perfunctory kisses, thanking us for our hospitality and company.

My wife was planning to visit family with the kids that entire week. I was to attend to job and home. They hadn't seen her parents, who live a three-hour drive away, in over a year. I had no objections at all. I helped pack and load up the car, saying, "Drive carefully" to my wife and admonishing my kids. "Be good at Grandma's and Granddad's."

I went inside and made some lunch. I consumed half the afternoon with chores.

At three o'clock the doorbell rang. I thought it was probably some collector for charity. Frankly I was annoyed at the interruption. I scowled as I opened the door, and then my jaw dropped.

It was Annette.

She asked, "May I come in?"

"Why, Annette!" I said in clutched surprise, swallowing hard. "Yeah, of course." My thoughts were racing. I restrained them, for fear of frustration. Might I have misread events? Quickly I said, "Sure," stepping back, beckoning her delectable form through the door. I added, "Is something wrong?"

She stepped inside, her hiking boots falling heavily against the tiles, and she kept her eyes from mine. I closed the door behind her. She took two steps toward the living room, then must have realized she still had on her hiking boots. She said, "Madame and the boys went to Grandmama's, no?"

I said, "Yes." My dick was thinking predictable things.

Annette turned and looked me full in the eyes. She said, "I had to come back, Bill." She stepped toward me. I was frozen in place, my arms stiff as boards. "Can you please, Bill, touch me some more, as you were?"

Her tone was pleading. I stepped forward, put my arms

around her and kissed her. She trembled, emitting soft cries of delight. We struggled with her boots, and I carried her upstairs to the bedroom.

We took a lot of gentle time that afternoon, that evening and night. After undressing her, I caressed and licked her to a moaning, shouting crescendo, avidly licking her clit, darting my tongue into and around her. Afterward she urgently guided me inside her, where I exploded immediately. I remained. She rocked, she rolled, I stayed hard. One quality I value most about a woman is the rhythm she uses while fucking, her moans and sounds. I call it her "love song." All women are different. Discovering that rhythm is a lot of fun. For me, it's the secret to staying hard and squirting them full of come twice, thrice. Annette's French-accent love song was beautiful, with her "Ah, hah, ooh, mah, cons, cons!"

I woke the next morning about half past six, running a bit late for getting to work by quarter to eight. I left Annette slumbering, naked. I did it with some hesitation and desire. My cock was getting hard again just from looking over her in deshabille, her firm ass, recalling how I stroked it, how she rubbed it against my prick in a tease, her disheveled hair, and her salacious, satisfied smile. I took a shower, went to another room, got dressed and skipped downstairs, where I quietly fixed myself some breakfast. I left breakfast out for Annette, along with a note suggesting that she reheat it.

I was readying to leave when I saw pretty, white feet padding down our center stairway, followed by adorable, freckled legs. Annette was dressed in one of my white shirts, open in the front, and nothing else. I kissed her hello, explaining how I had to go, arms wrapped around her. She kissed back warmly. I frowned, saying, "I'm sorry, Annette, I *have* to be at work today. I'm looking forward to this evening, though, very much."

Annette said, "Yes, I understand. You must work." Then she stepped back a half step, thinking, smiling to herself. She said, "I think I give you something so you cannot forget me before this evening no?"

I couldn't imagine what she had in mind. Having learned that her ability to innovate sexually was exquisite, I was definitely not going to discourage her. She undid my black leather belt, slowly zipped down my fly, and dropped my dress pants to the floor. At this point, I started to grow. She knelt and pulled my briefs, sliding them down ever so slowly. I was rock hard, pointing outward. She rose from her knees and padded over to the kitchen table. She picked up a saucer, spooned some marmalade into it, and returned.

She knelt again, smiled sweetly at me, and dipped a long-nailed index finger into the marmalade, bringing the coated red-painted nail to her open lips, and sucking it off. "Hmm . . . it is good," she commented sensually. She repeated the dip, but this time she daubed the jelly over the top of my dick. She got some more, and put it farther down the shaft. She put down the dish and gently, expertly, began to smear the jelly all over my manhood. I just spread my legs apart and enjoyed the sensations, the moments when her nails touched my sensitive skin, making me jump, and her giggle.

Then, with a sigh, she knelt, opened her mouth, and started to lick up the marmalade. She did it very slowly and gently, not wanting to miss the slightest bit. At first I could hardly tell she was touching me at all, but the mere idea drove me crazy. She cooed, "How you say, 'Yum'?" We laughed together as she continued. I must tell you, as this went on and on for fifteen minutes, Annette saw me quivering, shaking, reduced to utter helplessness at her actions. *Anyone* could have come into the house at that moment and I wouldn't have cared. Annette was my universe. My cock exuded drops of come. Annette said, "Bill, you are delicious." She smiled at me devilishly. "Now for the breakfast," she said, opening her mouth, and took me into it, her tongue working underneath the head. She turned hers slightly, and simply sucked, no longer moving about, but sucking hard, wet, warm. I was buzzing with desire, and my dick felt like it would explode. I gave a great trio of groans when I came, spurting into her mouth like a fire hose.

I thanked Annette and went off to work. You can guess what I thought about during the drive. A buddy of mine pointed out that I must have dropped some marmalade on my slacks during a hurried breakfast. I almost laughed, but I caught myself, and said, "Yes, I'll have to take it to the cleaners."

It was genuinely hard to keep focused on work all day. I think the moment with Annette I recalled the most was a quiet time very early in the morning when she cuddled her head against my shoulder, stroking the hair on my chest. I daydreamed about that through lunch. I think every satisfying encounter has a moment when you look in each other's eyes and realize the lovable, sharing, giving being behind them. This was Annette's moment, or rather, mine of her. I got out of work at five that night, eager to go home.

As I unlocked the door, I called, "Annette," but there was no answer. I checked through the mail and dropped my coat and briefcase. I called again, "Annette?" She could have gone out for a walk, but I got an uneasy feeling that I'd find some kind of remorse-filled note in the bedroom.

I walked into the bedroom, and, seeing a feminine form in the bed, covers pulled up over her head, thought that my questions had been answered. "Oh," I said, "there you are," but realized she might be sleeping. Quietly, I got undressed and lifted the quilt, sliding under it. As I approached the warm body. I put my hand on her hip, stroking the top of her ass. She lifted her head and turned to me, long blonde hair covering the pillow and tops of her shoulders. This was not Annette.

"But . . ." I said. "Where's . . .?"

My mystery woman smiled, leaned forward and kissed me, pressing her softness against me. I returned the kiss, still wondering, but enjoying the surprise. I kissed her neck, then shoulders, sliding down to lick and caress large, white breasts, looking like whipped cream-topped sundaes with cherries melted atop them in a cranberry sugar sauce. She sighed and oohed. As I touched and licked, she moved her left hand lazily about my chest, down my side, along my taut abdomen. She moved a warm palm down a leg to the front of my thighs, encountering my stiffness by happenstance. She stroked her discovery as I gently nibbled and circled my tongue about her nipples, almost tasting the cranberries. She lifted a leg and wrapped it about mine, hugging me closer to her, slipping her free hand to the small of my back.

I kissed between her breasts, her stomach, saying how beautiful, how delightful she was. She said, "Bill, I'm dripping," with a heavy French accent. She knew my name! *Her* name was Miou, I learned later. She lived only a few blocks away. Annette had given her the key. But at that point I was too unruly with passion to think about explanation. She opened her legs like a butterfly might its wings, yielding her pink warmth to me. I first admired and touched her cunt, her silvery mound of hair. I found her clit among ample folds, kissing either side of the opening with long tongue, then making for it, seeking shelter from the storm. I gradually converged at the top, gently eating, sucking, twirling her pink button, saying, "Hmm, yum," delighting in her taste. She was indeed wet, and had a familiar, natural-smelling fragrance about her. She was hot, for she crested in no time, muttering incomprehensible, wonderful-sounding French words.

She took my head in her hands, and led me over her, impaling herself with me. Miou flipped me over, still inside her, and sat on top of me, crisscrossing her legs. She began to move her pelvis about, rocking me and spinning my prick, pumping up and down so the bed began to shake. She stared blankly ahead, focused upon the sensations. I felt like my dick was an inflating balloon, and I did my share of rocking, trying to reach as many parts of her insides with it as I could. Our rhythm went up, around and down, pushing, relaxing, pushing, pushing. Miou breathed out with a slight cry, then repeated it, "Ahh-eh, ahh-eh!" getting more insistent each time. I groaned loudly. I blew off, arching my back, digging my heels into the bed with the tension. She kept pounding as I settled back, and then threw her head and her hair back with a jerk, groaning as the waves of pleasure rolled over her, compensating her for her efforts. She collapsed on top of me, and we slept almost immediately.

What was special about Miou? She made me feel very male, even by sleeping there, white sheet intertwined and twisted seductively about a leg, half covering her pubic hair, pelvis, and a single breast. I watched her charms move up and down with her gentle breathing. In the window-framed moonlight she looked like some Venetian goddess. I got up to use the bathroom and get water. I pulled on my briefs, out of habit and for comfort. As I walked about, I felt I was all balls and dick, as if these organs were volumes bigger than I realized. I was so conscious of them, so happy I could delve and thrust and shake and rub Miou with my dick, shoot her full of jellied jism, and that she was delighted with my doing so.

Work the next day was even harder that the one previous.

On the way home, I stopped by an organic-food store to pick up some bread and things. There was an "Under New Management" sign on the outside. I found what I wanted, and then waited by the register, ringing the bell there. When no one appeared, I just walked about, killing time. They were probably out back in the warehouse, unloading, I thought. Ten minutes went by, and I started to get impatient. I found a door leading to the dock and opened it, softly calling, "Hello?" I heard vaguely familiar sounds from within. I took a cautious step forward. I peeked around a corner and saw a naked, dark-haired, handsome young man, eyes closed and mouth open in pleasure. Annette was kneeling at his feet, naked and tan, her firm ass resting on her heels. She caressed his hairy legs. She had his long prick in her mouth. Then she took it out, licking it slowly along its long shaft to the bottom, and then back again. She didn't put her mouth over it, just worked her dark pink tongue over its very tip, over and over, lapping up pre-come, saying teasing words in French to the one she was pleasuring. There were clothes scattered on the ground. I stayed quiet, observing, enjoying the voyeurism. My dick grew again, and I was tempted to jerk off, or even to join them. But instead I just watched.

The man—whose name I later learned was Gerard—opened his eyes and reached down for Annette's shoulders. Gerard is very strong. He's not at all heftily built, but he is tall, all bones and muscle. He lifted Annette to his shoulders, one leg over each, Annette's pubes before his face, and began eating her out. Annette stroked Gerard's hair. I was fascinated by the torrid scene before me.

Gerard let Annette down gently and lashed her nipples with his tongue. Gerard then kneeled and directed Annette to kneel as well. His very hard dick stood up like a flagpole as he leaned backwards. Annette stepped astride of Gerard. She took his straight prick within her, her legs far apart, and began to move up and down. He groaned once, exhaling some indescribable words.

This was quite a scene. Annette rocked up and down on Gerard's dick, loving it, beating herself to a climax. She and Gerard came within a half-minute of each other, Gerard finally collapsing onto his back on the floor.

Rising, Gerard took Annette in his arms, thanking her and kissing her. He pulled up his trousers, and Annette started getting dressed. I ducked back into the main store and waited by the cash register.

Gerard came out, and with a heavy French accent said, "I'm sorry I kept you waiting." I said there wasn't a need for apologies. I said it was well worth the wait. He looked at me, puzzled. Annette came around the corner, only half-dressed, her shirt still open, showing braless breasts. She had recognized my voice.

I said, "Annette, how have you been?"

Annette smiled and explained the whole story. She had taken a long walk through the neighborhood, and found the organic store. She stopped in to shop, and found Miou behind the register. Quickly Annette discovered that Miou spoke French, and was in fact from France, having moved here recently with her husband, Gerard. They were both happy to have found someone from home, and rapidly exchanged gossip. Miou confided that she was disappointed with American men, at least during her short time here. She knew some that would love to bed her, but they were too shy. In France, she explained, she found several satisfying, extramarital engagements. Gerard, she said, approved, even joined in once with a man and his wife. He thought it kept their bed life alive.

Annette told Miou she knew of an American man who would treasure her, if only she could make it with Miou's adorable husband. Miou smiled slyly, Annette said, much to Gerard's surprise and pleasure—he was hearing this for the first time too—and heartily agreed. Annette gave her the keys to my house. Miou ended up in my bed, and Annette spent the night with Gerard.

I get a postcard from Annette from time to time. She's married now, and has a kid on the way. Gerard and Miou still own the organic-food store, and I see them once or twice a year. Gerard and I still share Miou and she loves it. *Vive la femme! Vive la France!*

A Soldier's Story

The air force had canceled my reservations at their posh hotel. Baggage in hand, I headed for the nearest motel.

I ended up making a slight detour to the NCO club, where I bumped into a married couple I'd met the night before. The man was personable, in his late forties, and blessed with an attractive wife who was many years younger than he. Despite her looks, I didn't like her. After watching her in action, I'd decided she was nothing more than a prick tease.

While exchanging pleasantries, I told them about how I had been bumped by the air force and had no place to stay that night. They immediately offered the use of their couch. "I don't want to impose," I told them, but they insisted. After a while I accepted their offer, even though I wasn't crazy about the lady.

Arriving at the apartment, my host said he was going to take a shower and go to bed. I found myself alone with his young wife. We had a long, animated, sometimes hostile conversation until the wee hours. I was still not impressed.

The next day we went to the club again. Returning to the apartment, my host again announced he was going to shower and retire. His wife also took a shower, while I watched television. She returned wearing only a skimpy robe. She sat next to me on the couch and brushed her hair. I offered to do the honors. She had beautiful hair. It smelled delicious. As I gently ran the brush though her locks, I became increasingly aware that she was smoothly naked under the thin robe.

Our conversation drifted to more sensual topics. I realized she was rather sensitive underneath her tough exterior. She wasn't the coldhearted person I had originally pegged her to be.

Difficult as it was, I kept the beast in my pants in check. After all, I was their guest.

After she went to bed, I lay in the moonlight thinking about the situation. Then, out of the corner of my eye, I saw an almost ghostlike image. It was her, in a gossamer chiffon negligee, almost transparent in the moonlight.

Before I could move or speak she placed her warm, moist lips against mine. Her passion flowed into me, spreading and warming. Then, just as suddenly as she appeared, she was gone.

I lay there on the couch for what must have been thirty minutes. My pulse was pounding, my body feeling as if it had been electrified. Confused, a thousand questions raced through my mind. Finally, I decided I had been right. She was a prick teaser. I was angry. Angry at her, but also angry at myself. I *wanted* her. I wanted her so bad.

The next day we again went to the club, and again returned to the apartment. True to form, my host announced he was going to take a shower and retire. She, on the other hand, said she needed some things at the store. Her husband tossed his car keys to me and asked if I'd drive her. A little reluctantly, I said, "Sure." I wasn't in a hurry to have her light my fire again, especially when I knew she wasn't going to cook anything.

Silently, we walked outside and got into the car. I started the engine and headed toward the street that would take us into town, where she could get bread, milk and a few other things she needed. Neither of us spoke while I drove. I kept replaying the events of the night before, trying to figure out what kind of game it was that she was trying to play with me.

Then I felt her gently place her hand on my knee. Not taking my eyes off the road, I savored the feeling of her palm firmly pressed against me, running up and down the length of my leg from knee to crotch.

"You're probably wondering about last night," she said.

"You got that right." I answered. "I really don't appreciate being teased like that. And," I impatiently brushed her hand off my knee, "do me a favor and cut the crap before you go and give me another hard-on like last night."

"Did I do that?" she asked.

"What the hell do you think?"

I heard her let out a sigh. "I'm sorry for getting you angry," she said. "It's just that I wanted you so bad. I had to just . . . just kiss you. I didn't want to risk my husband walking in on us."

"Your husband isn't here now, is he?" I asked. I let my remark hang in the air as I pulled into the parking lot of an all-night convenience store. I shut the car off and we both sat in silence, neither of us making a move to get out.

I felt her fingers fumbling with my belt. Then she was undoing my fly. I lifted my ass off the seat so she would be able to pull my pants and underwear down. My cock was already stiff when she took it in her cool hand. She lowered her head and gently took my cock into her moist mouth.

I closed my eyes and let my head fall back against the headrest as she gave me head there in the car. She took her time, licking my entire cock, sucking just the head, gently cupping my balls in her hand.

"Hey, you're pretty damn good at this," I said.

She didn't take her mouth away to reply, and I didn't mind one bit. I felt an orgasm approaching as the hot come sizzled in my balls. Faster and faster her mouth rose and fell on my cock. My pubic hair was soaked with her saliva. I grunted and shot my load into her mouth. I was thankful that she didn't pull away, and instead drank my come.

I am not sure how it happened. The next thing I knew we were standing alone in a dark motel room. We didn't speak. Slowly, I walked toward her and took her in my arms for the first time. If this was a tease, it was a good one.

I knelt and slowly began to remove her clothes. She started to speak, but I put my fingers to her lips. I didn't want words to shatter the moment.

I'd never really paid attention to her body, but as each layer of clothing was pulled away, I became more interested. Her skin was satiny smooth and pale in the failing light. Her breasts were full and round, with hard nipples that begged to be kissed. I slowly rolled down her panties, unveiling a rich, lush pelt, scant inches from my face. The subtle fragrance was headier than any exotic perfume. I looked up and she seemed embarrassed, unsure. My prick-teasing vixen was, in reality, a shy little girl.

Quickly shedding my clothes, I took her in my arms. This time it was my kiss that held her passion. Her skin was warm, smooth and soft as it pressed against me. My prick was begging to slide between her creamy thighs, but I held off. I wanted this to last a long time. She needed to understand that teasing is not nearly as good as pleasing.

I carried her to the bed and laid her gently on the crisp, cool sheets. Her dark hair framed her beautiful face. Her soft brown eyes were filled with uncertainty. She tried to cover herself modestly. Slowly, I explored her body with my lips and tongue. From her gentle forehead to her toes I licked, sucked and kissed every nook and cranny.

She threw her head back and her body started shaking when my tongue lightly grazed her hard clit. The lips of her cunt were slick with her love, and her natural perfume filled the room.

She was the first woman I'd ever met who had a truly beautiful pussy. It was almost a work of art. Up till that night, I had only feasted on a woman to be obligatory. But with her it was a labor of love. She was so sweet and silky. With each stroke of my tongue, her body arched and quivered. Her moans became louder and her hands urged me on.

Sliding up her sweating body, my rock-hard dick pressed against her stomach. She looked at me, her eyes pleading for me to make passionate love to her. I slowly raised my body and moved my cock between her thighs. I placed the blood-engorged head against her moist, velvety thatch.

I smiled and asked her if she wanted me to put it inside. She nodded.

"No, baby," I said. "I want to hear you say it."

Her words seemed to drip with passion. "I want to feel you, all of you, deep inside me."

Slowly, I lowered myself into her. I could feel her muscles holding me, rippling as, ever so slowly, I started long, deep thrusts. I wanted this to last, it was too good to rush. She, despite her apparent naiveté, was a natural lover. She moved with ease, matching my every stroke.

We began to move faster, her body and hands urging me on. Her lips left a trail of wet fire on my neck. Faster and faster, I could feel the pressure building. As I raced toward the finish, my dick burned with anticipation, my balls sizzling as they filled with hot come. I knew I wouldn't be able to hold off much longer.

Suddenly she gave a loud moan and held me tight. Her hips thrust up, burying me deep inside. I felt her cunt spasm.

It was then that my dick exploded inside her, pulsing with

each spurt. It felt as if my whole body was draining into her through the head of my dick.

We collapsed. Our bodies were covered with sweat. We lay there for a while, just looking at each other. Then, gently, she gave me a little kiss.

For two days we explored. Hot-oil massages, steamy showers—the list of what we did is endless. We wrapped ourselves in sensuality, completely forgetting about everything else. Finally, it had to end.

I couldn't let her go back to face the music alone, so I decided I'd go with her to her husband.

When we arrived at the apartment, it was empty. I mean empty! Not a piece of furniture, not even a scrap of paper, was left.

Beth and the Frat Boy

I saw one of my fraternity brothers talking to a carful of fellow students in the parking lot behind the house. There were two attractive women in the car. I thought the blonde in the backseat was especially sexy, so I gave her a smile. Her name was Beth, and as she tipped her sunglasses farther down her nose to give me a view of her luminous green eyes, I imagined how she might look in sunglasses alone: a smooth, silky body begging for my tongue. Thank goodness my fraternity brother and I were late to class. If I'd stayed any longer, I would have embarrassed myself by getting a pulsing hard-on.

I mentioned to my fraternity brother that I thought Beth was hot. I needed a date to our formal the following weekend, and he said Beth was definitely available, so I called her that evening. We talked for half an hour before I asked her to the formal. I told her what a great time we were going to have—the party atmosphere, the great tunes, the booze and the wild dancing. Her voice sounded soft, sexy and deep, and I began to rub my dick through my shorts while talking to her.

The day of the formal was pretty wild. As is the tradition at our fraternity, we have a celebration before the dance. We were doing shots of tequila—lots of shots—and playing touch football. I had wisely gotten dressed before I got too drunk: I knew what it was like to be in such bad shape you can't even tie the laces of your shoes! Now I had a great buzz going and could barely see the passes I was catching.

Before I knew it it was nine o'clock. My tux was stained from the football game, but it was too late to get another one. I ran across campus to Figman Hall, which was Beth's dorm, and knocked on her door. I had a big smile on my face and smelled like a man: cologne and sweat, grass, dirt and tequila. Thank goodness I was chewing a piece of mint gum. The door opened and a little brunette said Beth would be right out and asked if I wanted a beer. I had no willpower. "Sure," I said.

Beth came out with a big smile on her face and said, "I'm excited about the party tonight." She had wavy blonde hair with some extra mousse in it to make it really stiff. She had a light, flawless complexion and the cutest little nose which turned up at the end. It reminded me of my penis, which was starting to get erect.

Beth was wearing a black party dress cut way above her knees. She had on a silver-gold belt revealing a small waist, and she wore no bra to cover her firm breasts. Her nipples were hard and pointing out. I gave her a kiss on the cheek and hugged her so that I could savor those luscious melons pressing against my chest. I felt a tremor in my crotch, but was still too drunk to get a real hard-on.

We walked in the front door of the fraternity house, and I took Beth's hand and led her down the stairs into the basement where we have our parties. We went immediately to the bar, and I got Beth a gin and tonic that was mostly gin. I poured myself a gin with no tonic at all. This was a party! We sipped our drinks and started to talk about school, our voices barely able to penetrate the loud music. A few minutes later the disc jockey began played a really good tune. Beth and I put our drinks down and headed straight to the dance floor. I looked at her glass and noticed she'd practically sucked down the entire drink.

The next song was a slow one. Beth pulled me close and put her arms around my neck. I put one hand on her back and the other right above her perfect ass. As the song progressed, I concentrated on pressing my body tightly against hers. Her tits were making their presence known, and to my delight she gyrated her hips ever so slightly against my crotch. I took that as a hint, moved one of my hands to her ass and started to rub with vigor. We must have been putting on quite a show, because most of the other couples had stopped dancing and were watching our passion ignite.

Not wanting to be an exhibitionist, I suggested we take a break. I looked right at her crotch, then into her lustrous green eyes. She looked back at me and ran her tongue seductively across her upper lip. No words needed to be spoken. I grabbed her hand and half-led, half-pulled her through the throngs of people as we made it up the three flights of stairs to my room. As I was trying to unlock the door she reached under my ass, between my legs, and tickled my scrotum with her long fingers. She played with my balls with such delicacy that it made me shudder with delight. I leaned over and kissed her deeply, my tongue practically reaching her tonsils. I was so excited that I had a hard time getting the key in the door. She had to steady my hand with hers. I turned the lock and rushed into the room. I reached around and locked the door securely.

I grabbed her arm and pulled her to me, caressing her ass and pulling her crotch to mine. The effects of the alcohol were diminishing and I was sporting a lively boner. Beth glided her crotch over my ice-hard dick, moving in a circular motion so intense I thought she would split the seams of my trousers. She broke away from our long, deep kiss and went to work on my ear, slurping and sucking it like she was trying to make it come!

Beth was working both of us into a frenzy. I massaged her braless tits while rolling and pinching the nipples with my fingers. She leaned over, blew warm air into my ear and whispered, "I'm so horny I can't stand it." While still tongue-fucking my ear, Beth took her right leg and hooked it around my back, shifting most of her weight and practically jumping on me. I kissed her again and told her I was going to make her come until the sun came up. She moaned and replied, "Oh, I can't wait to feel your cock!"

I felt her cunt through her black dress while undoing her belt. Beth undid my shirt, slowly at first, then ripping it off me so that the buttons popped off and shot across the room. She reached into my briefs and massaged my cock, playing with the pre-come that had oozed from the tip. I kicked off my trousers and shoes, and quickly whisked away my socks while Beth tossed her clothes behind her. We stood skin-to-skin, except for our briefs, kissing each other and working our hands feverishly, unable to get enough of each other.

I kneaded her breasts and started sucking her nipples. Beth's areolae were the size of silver dollars and her nipples were as hard as my dick. I left her saliva-coated nipples and moved up to her neck. We began to grind our crotches together, dry-humping to the music our hormones were providing. Beth ran her long fingers down my back. I was getting goose bumps all over my body.

By now the strong, sweet aroma coming from the patch of wetness between her thighs permeated the air. In a voice hoarse and full of passion, she looked straight into my eyes and said, "I want you to fuck me. I want to feel your cock inside me. I want you to . . ."

Before she could say another word I slid two fingers into

her sopping cunt. I pulled off her panties and used a third finger to jiggle her clit. I worked it in a circular motion, making her gasp and squeal as she rode my hand with gusto. Beth stiffened and then moved again, stiffened and moved again, keeping up this stop/start routine until she came. The amount of liquid that shot out of her was unbelievable. I'd never known a woman could ejaculate like that. My parents were right. College was full of learning experiences.

I pulled my fingers out so I could taste her honey, then put them near her mouth so she could also have a taste. She sucked my fingers the way I hoped she could suck cock, giving them long, wet licks and taking them deep into her throat. We fell to the floor, the fires of our lust raging. She lay on her back and spread her legs far apart, knees up. I stroked my dick, hovering over her mouth.

"Do you want it?" I asked.

"Yes, yes!"

"Where do you want it?" I teased, lowering myself until my cock was just out of reach of her lips. She snapped at it, trying to take it into her mouth, but I quickly pulled it away. She giggled and tried again, but again I kept her from tasting the knob of my cock.

"Please give me your cock. I want it now," she said. I looked down to see she was pumping a finger in and out of her pussy. What a turn-on!

"I know what you really want," I said. "You want it in your pussy, don't you?"

"Yes."

"Tell me about your pussy, Beth. Tell me what it's like."

"It's hot, sticky, and very wet," she began.

"And tight?" I asked.

"Tight as a fist," she said. "It's going to squeeze all the come out of you."

"That's good," I said, "because—"

But before I could finish, she grabbed my cock and stuffed it inside her. "Enough talking!" she said. "Just fuck me, baby!"

Her cunt felt so good around my bulging cock and I wanted to savor the feeling. I held her still for a second, letting the incredible heat of her pussy consume me. She locked her legs around my back and pulled me deeper into her. Her pussy felt like the mold where my dick had been cast—a perfect fit. I pressed my mouth to hers, feeling her erect nipples press into my chest. The continual slurping sounds of my dick plunging in and out of her moist cunt filled the room.

I was really putting it to her, so at first I didn't hear the knocks at the door. But as the pounding grew more insistent, it dawned on me that my roommate, Mel, wanted in. Beth and I were almost at the pinnacle of pleasure too. Damn! I covered her beautiful body with a sheet, grabbed a towel to cover my swollen, throbbing dick and, with a scowl, answered the door.

Mel stared back at me, his girlfriend at his side. They looked desperate, like they really needed a place to fuck—I guess her room was unavailable. I told them to come back in a while, then motioned to Beth to let them know I wasn't alone.

"We don't mind," said Denny, Mel's girl. "It could be a party." Denny was a hot number and at any other time I would have jumped at the chance to be in the same room while she was fucking Mel. But I'd just met Beth and didn't want anyone else around, at least not for a little while longer.

"Come back in an hour," I said. Drunk, horny and disappointed, Mel and Denny left.

I went back to Beth, apologized for the interruption and resumed kissing her. I couldn't wait to finish what we'd begun. But I must have been drunker than I'd thought, because all of a sudden the room started spinning. I mean really spinning. I had to lie down on the floor.

"Are you okay?" Beth asked.

"Just give me a minute," I said. It was right about then, I guess, that I blacked out.

I don't know how much later it was when I awoke, but I knew I'd been out for some time. My head was still spinning too, but for a different reason. Beth, naked and gorgeous as ever, was lying on her stomach, her face buried in my crotch. Her wet mouth was busily sucking my hard cock. I had blacked out many times, but I'd never been revived like this before! She gave a playful blowjob, flicking at the head with her pink tongue and taking long, lollipop licks at the shaft. My dick felt like a red-hot poker sitting in a fire.

"Oh good, you're back," she said when she saw me stir. "I was hoping that would do the trick." Satisfied with my recovery, Beth changed positions and straddled me, lowing herself seductively on my cock. "You said something about making me come until the sun came up. We still have a few hours left." With that, she impaled herself on my sausage.

Beth rolled her hips, filling herself with every inch of my prick and rubbing her clit against me. She moved from side to side and up and down, like some wild carnival ride. I could see the orgasm building up inside her. Her hips bucked faster and her head was tossing left and right. "Fuck me, fuck me!" she said through deep breaths. "Deeper! I want it deeper!"

I grabbed her ass and pulled her to me as tightly as I could. She told me to suck her titties, and that did the trick. No sooner had I taken her left nipple between my lips than she screamed, "Yes! Oh yes, come with me!"

Beth slithered up and down my cock, milking out my load as it exploded into her. The feeling was exquisite, and the sight of her riding up and down my pole kept me hard long enough to ram her to another pair of orgasms. She didn't stop moving, but instead urged me on by planting her luscious tits in my mouth. Finally, her back arched and she came again, her entire body crashing down onto my chest.

We regained our strength enough to get dressed and vacate the room for Denny and Mel. We made our way to Beth's dorm, hoping her roommate wasn't in so the night wouldn't have to end.

Bahamas Getaway

A few months ago while on vacation in the Bahamas, I had an experience that left no doubt in my mind why French women have such a reputation as expert practitioners of the art of love. I was staying at a small, very private resort hotel on one of the outer islands that attract very little of the usual tourist trade. The hotel accommodated only about twenty-five people. Each evening, the management offered a dinner seating for its guests in an elegant dining room with a magnificent view of the pink, coral-sand beach below.

It was our first night there. My friends and I were well into our second round of before-dinner cocktails when the sexiest, most gorgeous woman I have ever seen in my life strolled into the room and seated herself at an adjacent table. This woman was in a class by herself. Tall and slim, with the lean, muscular look of an athlete, she had dark, lustrous, shoulder-length hair and penetrating blue eyes. She was wearing red nylon running shorts just tight enough to show off a perfect ass, and a transparent white blouse through which I could easily see the dark circles of her nipples.

Throughout dinner my cock was twitching like crazy, as though it could sense the the world-class pussy of the woman sitting at the next table. I couldn't help but stare at her. She was talking with the three women and two men with whom she was dining. They all were speaking English with distinct French accents. I offered a silent prayer of thanks when, from the scattered bits of conversation I overheard, I figured out that she was not romantically involved with either of the men.

Several times during the meal she glanced over, caught me watching her and smiled before looking away. Unfortunately she didn't show up later on in the cocktail lounge as I'd hoped she would. Disappointed, I lulled myself to sleep that night stroking my meat, dreaming about the far more interesting things I could be doing with her if she were in bed beside me.

Early the next morning I went for a run on the beach, then decided to cool off with a leisurely ocean swim. As I emerged from the water, refreshed, my prayers of the previous evening were answered. Coming down the stairs and heading for the beach, wrapped in a white terry-cloth robe, was the woman. I watched as she pulled a canvas beach chair closer to the water, dropped her sunglasses and keys onto it, then casually stepped out of her robe. I blinked several times, hoping to God that this wasn't just a dream from which I would wake up alone with my dick in my hand. It was real, though—she was standing there wearing only the tiniest bikini bottom.

My prick started to stiffen while I gazed at her full breasts swaying slightly as she walked into the water, and I nearly came on the spot when she turned away from me and bent over to get her hair wet, showing me the most glorious set of buns I had ever seen. I suddenly realized that this was no accidental meeting and that she knew exactly who I was and what she was doing. I began to have great difficulty keeping my seven-inch tool inside my tight swimsuit as I watched her move through the shallow water to where I was standing.

"*Bonjour*," she said. "I am Jeanette. Do you remember me from last night?"

"Hi, Jeanette, I'm Barry. And you've got to be kidding. Only a blind man could forget someone who looks as good as you do," I replied, trying my hardest to look at her face and not at the pair of perfectly shaped tits that were bobbing in and out of the water in front of me. "I didn't think a woman could look any sexier than you do. You really have a fantastic body."

"I'm so happy you like it," she said. I noticed her looking down through the crystal-clear water and realized she was inspecting the huge lump growing in my swimsuit. She was smiling when she looked back up and said, "It looks like you have some impressive features yourself." I felt her cup my balls in her hand and then trace a fingernail along the entire throbbing shaft of my cock. Before I knew what was happening she had pulled down my suit and was slowly stroking my hardness to full erection. As she continued to fondle me she said in a husky voice, "It's always an added treat to find out the man I've chosen is well-hung."

I wasn't exactly sure what she meant by "chosen," but I figured it couldn't be too bad if she'd planned to start the day by massaging my cock before breakfast. I put my arms around her and kissed her, taking a breast in my hand and feeling the nipple harden beneath my fingers. Moving to the smooth contours of her ass, I pulled her close to me, pressing my hard dick against her mound.

She moaned softly and moved against me with an urgency that was driving me crazy with lust. There was no doubt that if this continued for about two more minutes I was going to be standing waist-deep in the water no more than fifty yards from the shore, fucking this woman like a madman. As good as that sounded, I could see that there were now half a dozen people on the beach, all of whom were showing an interest in what was going on. I knew that, even in the Bahamas, there were a few things that could get you in trouble if you did them in public. So I disengaged myself from Jeanette, pulled my swimsuit back up and told her that we needed to continue this back at the hotel.

We made it back to her room in record time. The next thing I knew, I was sitting naked in a deck chair on her private balcony while she knelt between my legs and gave me what was probably the best head in the world. There is no other way to describe it. Jeanette made unbelievably hot, insane love to my cock with her lips and tongue. She'd take my entire length down her throat while gently squeezing my balls, and then with excruciating slowness would let my prick slide out of her mouth until just the big, purple head was inside her lips and she could caress the slit with the tip of her tongue. She seemed to be able to sense exactly when I was about to shoot my load. She would slow down, just lightly kissing the shaft or running the slippery head over her face until it was wet with my pre-come, then plunge it back down her throat. I'd never known anyone who had such a talent for giving head.

After about twenty minutes of this, my balls felt like they were going to explode if I didn't get some quick relief. "Honey," I moaned, "if you continue doing that I'm going to come like a volcano."

She paused momentarily, letting my cock slip out of her mouth, and looked up at me with a big grin on her face. "Barry, darling, you shouldn't worry. You are going to come many times today, as am I. This is only the first. You American men are always so concerned about the timing of your orgasms. Just relax and enjoy it. Believe me, I certainly intend to."

With that, she took my throbbing tool in her hand and began to jerk me off while at the same time flicking her tongue over the sensitive underside of my cockhead. I completely lost control at that point and started coming like a fire hose, shooting stream after thick stream of semen. She never missed a beat and kept steadily sucking on my schlong.

"Oh yes, baby, yes!" she cried. "God, I love watching a man shoot off like that. It turns me on so much I just can't stand it." She squeezed out the last of my jism and slowly licked it from the head of my cock. "Now I need to come, lover. Make me come, baby. Please eat my little pussy and make me come right now!"

She quickly stood up, turned around and bent over so her dripping cunt was right in my face. I went right to work, grabbing her hips and giving her sweet-tasting slit the tongue-job of my life. In about two minutes she went off like a rocket and let out a high-pitched wail that I was sure would bring the hotel manager knocking on the door. She bucked and wiggled so much that I had a hell of a time keeping my tongue on her lust-swollen clit. But it didn't seem to matter as she climaxed three or four times in succession, each one more intense than the last.

After a warm, lingering kiss on the lips, she grabbed my penis and gently tugged me up and out of the chair. "Time for a nice, hot shower," she said, and headed back into her room with me in tow. Inside, she gave my cock a squeeze and told me to get started while she ordered breakfast. I might add it turned out to be a hot shower in more ways than one. By the time we were done she had sucked me until I was stiff again, and then begged me to fuck her from the rear while the warm water cascaded down our bodies. I had been with some horny women before, but I was getting the idea that, as the day progressed, Jeanette was going to provide me with her own personal definition of "insatiable."

Later, over a leisurely breakfast on the balcony, Jeanette told me that she lived in Paris, near the Louvre, was married to a Swiss businessman and was in the habit of taking an annual, separate vacation—the sole purpose of which was to have great sex with a strange man. This was done with the full knowledge of her husband, who took a similar trip at the same time. She had chosen the Bahamas this year and he had picked Copenhagen where, as she put it, "some hot, blonde, Danish nineteen-year-old is probably fucking his brains out right now. And I hope he is loving it!" She said they both found it to be very beneficial to their marriage, kind of like getting their erotic batteries recharged once a year. Apparently she'd decided when she saw me at dinner that I was the sexual companion she wanted on this trip. I briefly wondered what I could have possibly done to deserve such luck, but by then I felt Jeanette's hand starting to stroke my prick again and decided to leave the analysis of my good fortune for another time.

The next three days were an unbelievable blur of nonstop sex. We fucked, sucked, probed, licked and touched in every way I could imagine, and in some I couldn't. We did it in bed, on the floor, on the beach at night, in the hotel pool, even in the ladies' room at the airport on the day we left. Jeanette acted like she just could not get enough of my cock. If it wasn't in her cunt, she had it in her mouth. And if not that, she was jerking me off with her hands or feet or having me fuck her between the tits. During those times when my dick was recuperating, she would sit on my face while I tongued her to orgasm after writhing orgasm.

When she kissed me good-bye at the airport, she told me to look her up if I ever found myself in Paris. You can guess where I'm planning to go on vacation next!

Box Lunch

When I met Victoria, I was thrilled to discover that we shared the same occupation. We drive eighteen-wheelers, hauling produce all over the country, so we ended up running together for a few months.

Victoria isn't your average trucker. She takes great pride in her appearance. Polished fingernails, perfectly done makeup and styled hair are part of her daily routine. She is about five foot four, one hundred twenty-five pounds, with silky-smooth skin and shiny, dark brown hair. She is very striking. We were really attracted to each other and soon we were involved in the most intimate relationship either of us has ever had. This story is about an afternoon tryst that was so hot that the recollection of it makes me rock-hard.

Last spring I had to take some time off from work due to health reasons. We had been apart for about three weeks and had spoken on the phone only a few times.

Early one morning I received a phone call from her. She told me that she wanted to go for a picnic lunch and canoe ride. I organized the afternoon with eager anticipation.

We met at one o'clock. I wanted to jump into the sleeper

of the truck right there and then partake of her fruits. She was wearing a pair of short cutoffs that showed the curve of her firm cheeks and a bright, red blouse. This only increased my desire for her. After she promised that she had something special in store for me, I was persuaded to wait.

The day was warm and sunny—not a cloud in the sky. We paddled along for about two miles. The lake was as smooth as glass. Suddenly Victoria stopped paddling and turned around in her seat, sliding to the floor of the canoe. She said that she was getting hot and undid all the buttons on her blouse. She opened her top just enough so I could see that she was wearing nothing underneath. She exposed a good portion of her breasts, letting the material just barely hide her nipples. By this point I was rock-hard and, as I was wearing only a bathing suit, little was left to her imagination. I really wanted to get the show on the road and diving into her muff would have been a great way to start, but she just sat there sunning herself. Occasionally she would massage her breasts and tweak her nipples, then she would slowly run her hands down her taut, flat stomach and under her cutoffs. She would leave her hands there for a moment or two, rotate her hips against her hands and then stop. I was going nuts with desire. Watching a woman play with herself is something that always turns me on.

I paddled to a spot by the cliffs. We parked the canoe and grabbed the gear that we needed for our lunch. There was a trail up the cliffs that led us to a very secluded spot overlooking the lake. Victoria said that this was our spot and started to lay out the blanket and organize everything. I gladly helped, knowing what was in store. I was ready to start my lunch. I figured a beaver sandwich would be a tasty appetizer. Victoria stood up and took her blouse off, then she seductively slid out of her cutoffs. She asked me to put some suntan lotion on her back, which I promptly did.

After taking care of her back, I worked my way down to her hips. Then I wrapped my arms around her, my oiled hands reaching for her breasts. After massaging her breasts until her nipples were as hard as bullets, I moved my hands down her tight stomach toward her love-nest. She pulled away, insisting that I run down to the canoe to get the cooler. Protesting that my cock was ready to explode, I reluctantly ran back to the canoe.

On the way back up the hill I heard moaning sounds coming from the area where I had left Victoria. When I got back to our site I saw a performance that I shall never forget.

Victoria was lying back on the blanket, her body glistening in the afternoon sun. She was well on her way to orgasm. I stripped out of my bathing suit, ready for action. Victoria was running her hands from her tits to her pussy, teasing herself. She rolled her oiled nipples between her fingers, then pulled them until they slipped out, hard and erect. Then she ran her hands down to her thighs, just above her knees. Her hands slid back up, right to her pussy lips. She pressed hard against her mons. Once more she slid her hands down her thighs, prying her knees apart and drawing them up. She drew her hands back up to her love triangle, moaning with pleasure. Slowly she began to gyrate against the pressure of her hands, building toward her climax. Sitting down at her feet I watched, trembling with excitement. She was too far gone to notice me.

With one hand she spread her lips. The other moved in unison with her hips as she fingered her clit. Suddenly she stopped. She took the finger that was doing all the work and stuck it in her mouth, sucking hard on it. When she drew it out, it was dripping wet with saliva. She reached down once more, this time sliding the finger up inside her cunt. At this point I could wait no longer. I leaned forward and dropped my tongue to her clit. She groaned and started coming. Although she had three quick orgasms back to back, I knew that she wasn't finished.

I knelt in front of her, grabbed my cock and rubbed the swollen head against her super-sensitive clit. She started coming again. I leaned forward and buried myself right to the hilt. She groaned with pleasure. After a few more strokes she came again. Just as she was at the peak, I exploded inside her.

After a few minutes of basking in our euphoria, she pushed me onto my back. Even though I was still fully erect, I was too spent to do anything. We lay side by side for a couple of minutes, then Victoria took over. She sat on my stomach, facing away from me, and started pumping my cock with her hands. Then she guided me back into her pussy, slowly moving her hips in a circular motion. This continued until I was ready to peak again. She stopped, sat upright, drew her knees up beside my hips and leaned forward. This gave me an excellent view of her pussy. With each stroke she took, her pussy lips pulled against my shaft, trying to suck every drop of come out of my cock.

With her pussy oozing, she began inching backwards toward my head. Although I had gone soft, the moment her pussy lips reached my tongue I was hard again. I stretched my tongue up to meet her clit and it was less than a minute before she was coming again. After she came she fell forward, totally exhausted. I ran my hands up her thighs and then slid them to her cunt, spreading her pussy lips apart. When I inserted two fingers into her hot twat, she started rubbing her face into my balls and stroking my cock.

She ran her tongue around the head of my swollen member. As I started rotating my thumb against her clit, she sank her lips down to the base of my cock. Then she spun around so I could watch the best blowjob in the history of mankind take place. After watching for a few moments, I was ready to pop again. Victoria sensed this and increased her speed. She massaged my balls and that was it. Groaning aloud, Victoria sucked every last drop out of me. After a while, we fell asleep in each other's arms. We slept for the rest of the afternoon.

When we woke up, we jumped into the crystal-clear lake. At dusk we headed back to the canoe and the mood for some more tender lovemaking overcame us. We made slow, gentle love in the canoe—the perfect way to end our perfect day.

Wild Strawberries

I'm a twenty-year-old male in the military. If there's such a thing as a food fetish. I've got it!

This happened about two years ago, and for as long as I live I will never forget it. I was living at home with my parents at the time.

It was Friday night. My parents had left earlier that evening and were going to be gone all weekend. I figured I'd have a party so I called a couple of friends and told them to come on over.

Pete and Dan showed up around nine. We started downing a bottle of tequila. About fifteen minutes later, Bernie showed up with Jane, a tall blonde with a nice body. After the introductions, I headed into the kitchen to mix two more drinks for the latecomers. Bernie followed me.

We talked while I prepared the drinks. "John, how would you like to give Jane the fucking of her life?" Bernie asked me.

Jokingly, I said, "You brought her, you fuck her."

He laughed and said, "No, I mean all four of us. Why not? We're all best friends, and she's one of the horniest women in town!"

I thought about this for a while, then said, "On one condition, I go first." He agreed.

After a few more drinks and some excellent smoke, I went into the kitchen and started making some preparations. Digging through the fridge, I grabbed three pounds of frozen strawberries and a few bananas. Next, I went to the garage and got some thick plastic bags to cover the bed with. When I was done, I went back into the living room to see how everything was going.

They were still sitting around. I whispered to Bernie that he should take Jane downstairs and help her to relax a bit.

As soon as they left, I threw the strawberries in the microwave to thaw them out. When I was done, Dan and Pete came in wearing shit-eating grins. Not long after that, Bernie came running up the stairs. He said, "She's ready." The three of them hurried back down. I was halfway down the stairs before I remembered the strawberries, so I had to run back up and get them. By the time I took them out, they were warm and squishy. I damn near got my rocks off just thinking about what was going to happen! Grabbing the fruit, I flew down the stairs, practically spilling the huge bowl of strawberries in the process.

I followed the trail of clothes to my bedroom. What I saw in there made my cock rock-hard. Jane was lying on her back with Pete's huge prick in her mouth. Her legs were spread invitingly and she was jerking Bernie and Dan off. I stripped as fast as I could, lit some candles and turned out the lights. I grabbed the bowl, walked over to the bed and started pouring. I began with her tits and worked my way down. She let out a muffled moan as the warm, sticky strawberries oozed down her stomach, slowly inching toward her mound. I emptied the last of the bowl onto her beautiful snatch. As I slowly spread her creamy thighs and started licking the strawberries off her pussy, she moaned and bucked, grinding her cunt into my face. She came at least twice. The four of us hungrily licked her clean.

I grabbed a banana, peeled it and slowly started to slide it into her wet pussy. She arched her back and thrust her hips forward to meet it. She went crazy as I fucked her with the banana. I was so into it, I didn't notice that the other three had left. When the banana was coated with her juice, I shoved it as far as it would go and started eating it out of her. I slid around into a 69, jammed my cock down her throat and fucked her mouth for all I was worth. It didn't take long for us to both come in one explosive orgasm.

We kissed and I rubbed the strawberries into her skin. She got a real laugh out of this, and she enjoyed it too. I scooped lots of the sticky fruit on top of her cunt and then I fucked her. My cock was nice and slippery from the strawberries, and I slid in and out of her like lightning. I popped one of her sticky, sweet-tasting nipples into my mouth, and I sucked it while I rode her hot box. When I was about to explode, I pulled out and shot my load.

Not long after that there was a knock at the door. Bernie came in saying, "My turn," and smiled. I could barely get up. I walked out and closed the door. I was covered with strawberries and squashed bananas and pussy juice, and I was thinking that this would be a weekend I'd never forget.

Since then I've tried various other foods—whipped cream, honey and butterscotch pudding. I want to try spaghetti, but I haven't yet found a willing partner.

Dutch Treat

When I joined the army last year I figured it would broaden my horizons. However, after I was promoted to lieutenant and learned I would be transferred to the Netherlands, I must admit I was apprehensive. I didn't know the language or the customs, and was afraid I'd feel alienated. But I soon learned that the Dutch were friendly people who liked Americans. Just how friendly they were I was soon to find out.

My story begins about two months after I arrived in Holland. It was a Friday night. I had been invited to join some Dutch officers for dinner and drinks. Since I knew I wouldn't be able to stay out too late, I opted to drive my own car. I followed them out to what I thought would be a local tavern. We drove through several small villages and down barren country roads. Finally we arrived at our destination. They bought me several mugs of my favorite beer, and soon we were laughing and joking. For dinner I ordered a hearty Dutch specialty, which I enjoyed immensely. After several hours of good food, good drink and good company, I said my goodbyes. I would have liked to stay with them for a while longer, but it was already after midnight and I had a full day of work ahead of me.

When I left the tavern, a terrible storm was raging. The night was black as ink, and the rain was coming down in sheets. I wasn't sure if I was going to be able to find my way home, but I was going to give it my best shot. After about thirty minutes of driving in what I had thought was the right direction, I realized I was totally lost. I couldn't even find my way back to the tavern.

I drove on, hoping to find an inn where I could get a room for the night. I was cruising along on a dark, narrow country road when I spied flashing lights ahead. My sagging spirits lifted—I figured that it was the neon sign of an inn or motel.

Much to my disappointment, the flashing lights turned out to be the emergency lights of a stalled camper. I pulled over to see if I could help. I climbed out, pulled my jacket over my head and went over to knock on the driver's window. No one responded to my knock. The camper seemed to be empty. Now, soaking wet as well as lost, I got back into my car and drove on.

Not too far down the road I spied someone moving along the side of the road. Obviously this was either the camper's owner or a local ghost. I pulled up alongside the ghostly specter and tapped on the window, beckoning to the person to get into the car. The door opened and a drenched figure wearing a bulky trench coat and a gray fedora climbed in. It was then that I realized my passenger was a beautiful young woman.

She caught my eye. We stared at each other for an eternal second. She finally broke the silence. With a smile she said, "Thanks for giving me a lift." She had a wonderful British accent.

"My pleasure," I gallantly responded. It appeared that my luck was beginning to change.

"Well, it's not a good night to be out in the rain," she proclaimed, "but it is a good night to be rescued by a handsome prince." This made me blush, which made her chuckle. Still blushing, I sheepishly admitted that I was lost and asked if she knew of a place to stay for the night. She replied, "I am also a stranger to these parts. We'll look for a place together." So the two of us drove on.

About five kilometers down the road we came upon a crossroads with a small farmhouse nestled off to one side. The lights in the house were all off, but we decided to stop anyway. The storm had started to let up a little. I got out and rang the bell. After several rings, a light went on and an old man answered the door.

I tried to explain that we had lost our way and needed a place to stay for the night, but the man didn't understand my English, nor my broken Dutch. I called to my companion to come help me out. She got out of the car and spoke to the man at length in Dutch. Evidently she finally convinced him of our plight, because he ushered us in out of the rain and up the staircase to the second floor.

He spoke to her again as he unlocked one of the rooms, then he left us. We entered and found a large antique featherbed, a dresser, a table and chairs, some towels and a washbasin. I looked around for another room or bed, but this seemed to be it. She was confused by my distress. "Where do I sleep?" I asked.

Pointing to the bed, she said, "Right there, of course."

"Well, where are you sleeping?" I responded.

Without blinking an eye, she said, "I'm sleeping there too. Will that be a problem?"

"No," I quickly replied.

She explained that this was not an inn, but a private home. The room we were in was a spare room that was used by relatives when they visited. She went on to explain that she had told the man that we were newlyweds, and he had taken pity on us, offering us a bed for the night, as well as a hot meal. "You see," she continued, "only if we were married would he have let us stay together in this room." Coyly she asked if she had done the right thing. My smile convinced her that I completely approved of her plan of action.

The tension in the air was broken by a knock on the door. The man's wife entered, carrying a tray with a steaming tureen, a pot of tea and some plates and mugs. She put the tray down on the nightstand, and my companion thanked her. The woman said good night and withdrew.

The tureen was filled with a thick, savory goulash. The tea was strong and sweet. "Let's eat before the food gets cold," I said, suddenly hungry.

"You eat. First, I'm going to get out of these wet clothes," she replied. As I ate, I watched as she took off her overcoat. She was wearing an emerald-green evening dress. It was still damp and clung tightly to her body. She was about five feet seven and one hundred twenty pounds, with medium-size breasts, a small waist and slender hips.

She hung the coat up and stopped to look at me. I was still staring at her. She smiled and pulled her gray fedora off. This unleashed a mass of lush auburn hair, which tumbled halfway down her back. Reaching behind her, she unzipped her dress and let it fall to the floor. I caught only a glimpse of lacy black lingerie before she wrapped a towel around her body. I immediately started to get a hard-on. Taking another towel, she patted her body dry and worked it over her damp hair.

I poured her some tea. She sat down across the table from me and brought the cup to her lips. A warm glow came to her cheeks as she sipped the steaming liquid. I got hard just watching her. She realized this and smiled, enjoying my discomfort. When I finished my stew she said, "You'll catch a cold if you don't get out of those wet clothes."

Not wanting to argue, I got up and moved over to the bed.

She watched, amused by the reversal of roles. I stripped to my briefs. It was obvious that, even from across the room, she could see the bulge straining against my briefs. As I reached for the last dry towel, she stood up and moved toward me. "It looks as if you could use some assistance drying off. Let me help you," she said. She took the towel from my hands.

She began to work vigorously on my body. As she rubbed, her towel came undone and fell to the floor, revealing a black, lacy, front-closing bra and matching bikini panties. I stared at her lovely globes, heaving with every breath. Constrained, they clearly longed to be free. I tested the waters by cupping a hand around one of those beauties and giving it a gentle squeeze. She smiled and moved closer. I deftly unfastened her bra. She shrugged the straps off her shoulders.

We kissed for the first time, timidly at first, then long and hard. She rested a hand on my ass and gave it a squeeze. Her breasts were hot against my chest. She moaned softly as I cupped her ass-cheeks and pulled her tightly against me. We moved in unison, our bodies pressed together. All that separated us from ecstasy were two pieces of terry cloth. She was dripping with passion. Gently I massaged her mound of Venus. Moaning with pleasure, she began the rhythmic dance of love.

Sliding her tongue from my mouth, she circled my erect nipples before gently licking them. My cock throbbed every time she moved. I sighed with pleasure. Her tongue cut a wet path down my chest. She slid my briefs off, then stopped, poised in front of my pulsing member. Making an O with her moist lips, she kissed the tip of my cock. Looking up at me, she said, "Now I want to thank you properly for rescuing me from the cold night." She slowly slid her lips over my electric rod. It was all I could do to just hold on.

When she pulled back, my cock emerged from her mouth

glistening wetly. But then her lips were tugging it again, taking in a little more each time until, finally, there was no more to take. I panicked with excitement. Beads of sweat were forming on my brow. I grasped her by the shoulders and guided her to her feet. Her lips glistened with pre-come and saliva. Her eyes were wild with passion.

"Not yet," I said. "It's too early to finish. Besides, now it's your turn." I kissed her long and hard. Our tongues searched each other out. I drew little circles around her erect nipples with my forefinger. They sparked with every touch, as if charged with static electricity. I pressed my lips around her nipples and tickled them with the tip of my tongue. She swooned, and I had to support her.

My strength waning, I slowly eased her down onto the mattress. Standing over her supine body, I slipped her panties off. Gently spreading her legs, I glided my engorged member into her waiting pussy. She was very tight, so progress was slow. I worked my cock in a little at a time. I was halfway in when she reached out and pulled me down on top of her, smothering me with kisses. Then, with one mighty thrust, I rammed my rod inside her to the hilt.

With a groan of passion, she whispered in my ear, "Fuck me. Fuck me hard." Bracing myself, I repeatedly slid my pulsing member in and out of her dripping pussy. She moaned softly as we both exploded in ecstasy. We lay intertwined, exhausted, until we fell asleep.

The next thing I remember was hearing a rooster crow loudly and seeing rays of sunshine darting through the windowpane. A knock on the door brought me completely to my senses. I suddenly realized I was in a bit of a predicament. You see, I usually wake up in the morning with a hard-on. Normally this is not a problem. However, we had fallen asleep in the same position that we had made love in, and now I found myself stuck inside my companion while someone banged on the door. I tried to pull out, but the juices of the previous night had dried up. My bedmate howled with laughter at my futile attempts. She reached for a mug on the night table and poured cold tea onto the problem area. The shock of feeling cold tea on my cock was enough to separate us.

I jumped to my feet, pulled on my pants and opened the door just a crack. I spied the same old woman from the night before with a breakfast tray. Pushing me aside, she entered the room, set the tray down and took the dinner plates away. My "wife" just sat there on the bed, naked, not saying a word. I looked at her in total disbelief, and we both burst out laughing. All she could say was, "Well, shall we eat?" After breakfast we made love again. Satisfied, we washed up and got into our clothes.

Finding the farmer, I thanked him for his kindness and paid him well. As we were leaving I looked up at our bedroom window and saw the old woman staring down at us. We waved and blew her a kiss. She smiled and waved back. I bet she was blushing a little. I know I was. We returned to my companion's camper and picked up some of her belongings, along with a few maps of the area. After we figured out where we were, I drove her home and headed back to my base. We see each other regularly now, and I am thinking of extending my stay overseas.

All Hands on Deck

No sexual experience I've ever had can compare to the one I enjoyed this past weekend. I had to write this as soon as possible because I don't trust my memory and if I wait to write I might leave something out. I certainly wouldn't want my husband to miss out on reading about my weekend fucking seven different men.

His favorite fantasy is to see me with other men, and I hadn't indulged him for a number of years.

My coworker Rachel had told me that part of my initiation to my new firm would be to let Herman, the owner, have a turn with me. After hearing her describe his equipment, I was definitely ready when Herman called and invited me on his boat for an overnight sail to the Cape.

On Saturday morning I packed a small bag, put on my new bathing suit under a pair of skimpy shorts and headed for the marina. My new suit is a white string bikini that shows off my ass. The top is a little too small, but I wanted to look as good as Rachel, who has one of those figures you wished you had—long legs, slim thighs, a tight butt and big tits. She has it all, but I've kept my five-foot-four body in great shape—and while I can't compete with her thighs, I definitely have her beaten in the boob department. My tits measure 37D and since I had kids, my nipples have become very big and prominent. I usually try to hide them, but not this day. I shouldn't have worried, because when I got to the boat I found only Herman, his partner Lou and a guy named Rob, whom I had never met. Herman told me that Rachel didn't feel well and had decided to stay home, but that I could handle her duties. "What duties?" I asked. Lou replied, "Drinks, drugs and decoration, what else?" He then laughed and introduced me to Rob. Rob was twenty-five and worked as a contractor. He had strong arms and hands to prove it.

Things got pretty busy then, and while the guys steered the boat I found a place to get some sun. I was dozing off when I heard Herman call for me. I went back and found the guys passing a joint. I asked, "Who's driving the boat?"

Herman said, "Don't worry about anything," as he passed me the joint. This stuff was powerful and hit me almost immediately. Pot affects me the same way as alcohol in that it really gets my juices going. I could feel my nipples expanding as I held the rich smoke in my lungs. After a few more hits I went below and brought up a pitcher of Herman's famous kamikazes. We were all having a great time, laughing and talking, when Lou said, "Well, I see drinks and drugs. Where's the decoration?"

Herman chimed in, "Yeah. Take off your shorts and let us see your ass."

I slowly stood up, unbuttoned my shorts and let them drop to the floor. "Okay?" I asked. There was silence for a long moment and I felt their eyes boring holes through me. Then Herman said, "You're beautiful, but we all have our shirts off and you're still wearing your top." He came over to me and, with one quick move, untied my top so it dangled from my breasts.

Lou grabbed one of the strings and slowly pulled it until

my top slid away and my tits were exposed to the guys' lustful gaze. "We have to be careful lest these beauties get sunburned," Herman said. He handed Rob a bottle of tanning oil and said, "Why don't you do the honors?"

With a sexy smile Rob slowly dripped the lotion onto my tits. "Does it feel good?" he asked. I could only nod as he slowly massaged my tits.

Every time he touched my nipples I felt an electric shock run straight to my pussy. I could feel the juices oozing from between my legs. I spread my thighs apart in hopes that one of them would get the hint, but it became obvious that these guys were pacing themselves. I knew then that the next twenty-four hours were going to be wild.

Herman and Lou left us to adjust the sails, but Rob stayed with me and continued teasing my nipples. By this time I was on the verge of orgasm, and couldn't stop myself from sliding my hand up his leg and wedging it into his crotch. I yanked his suit down, grabbed his cock and slowly pumped his shaft. He was really well-hung! His cock felt like a lead pipe in my hands and, as I squeezed him, a drop of pre-come blossomed at the tip. I smeared it all over his cockhead and was pleased to hear him groan at my touch. I pulled him closer to me so I could get him in my mouth and give him a blowjob. I sucked and licked him until he pulled away, saying that I was going to make him come too fast. I said, "You can always come again. Do it now." I sucked him into my throat until he shot his load. I could barely keep his seed in my mouth. His come dribbled out of my lips and dripped onto my breasts. He pulled out and smiled at me as I lay down to rest. When Herman came back he said to Rob, "You might as well keep your suit off, because you'll never get that big hunk of meat back inside." Rob laughed and said, "Not when she's around, that's for sure."

I knew I was acting like a slut, but I was too hot to care.

When Herman reached down and squeezed my pussy I thought I would come on the spot. Suddenly he took his hand away and dropped his shorts. His big cock dangled before me, begging to be eaten. Even soft, it was huge. The shaft was thick and heavily veined, and his balls were big, round and firm. My inspection of his magnificent cock was interrupted when I felt his fingers trace the outline of my pussy lips, pressing the nylon of my bikini into my damp slit. I opened my mouth, took his soft cock inside and licked him until he began to grow. It grew to such mammoth proportions there was no way I could hold it all. Soon only the head was in my mouth. His huge shaft stretched out a good eight or nine inches in front of me. I massaged his meat with both hands and it wasn't long before I tasted his come.

Lou approached me and asked if there was anything left for him. "Just her pussy," Rob said as he walked away. Rob stayed on deck as Herman and Lou took me below to Herman's cabin. Lou pulled off the rest of my suit and showed me his cock, which was the biggest I had ever seen. It was at least ten inches long and even thicker than Herman's. Lou knelt down to lap at my pussy while Herman nestled his dick between my tits. He was so big that every time he thrust forward I was able to take his cockhead into my mouth again. When I started to come, Herman pushed Lou out of the way and slowly pushed his cock into my pussy. I felt every heavenly inch as he stretched me wide open. My pussy had never felt so full. I wrapped my legs around him when he finally hit bottom. My clit tingled as orgasm after orgasm burst through me. He pulled out, then plunged back in and pumped harder and harder until I thought I would die from the pleasure. Suddenly I felt him stiffen. His cock throbbed as he pumped me full of come. When he pulled out I felt a rush of juice ooze down my leg. As he left the room he said,

"Why don't you catch some more rays before we really start to party?"

Lou kissed me and offered another joint, which I sucked on eagerly, but what I really wanted was more cock.

After I cleaned myself up, I went back up to the deck in only my bikini bottom. I spent the rest of the afternoon working on my tan while the guys worked on steering the boat and getting us all stoned. The pot was great and I felt totally relaxed, but my mind was filled with thoughts of sex. I thought about my husband—if he knew what I had been doing he probably would have invited his entire softball team over for a party. I could just imagine all those men wanting to fuck me, their hard cocks drooling in anticipation, pumping me until I came. The images were so vivid that I couldn't help but touch myself.

"Need some help?" I opened my eyes to see Herman standing before me, his long cock swinging between his legs. I smiled and reached for him, but he pulled me up and took me below, where Rob and Lou were preparing some snacks for cocktail hour.

Rob was naked and Lou's suit was so small it could hardly contain his cock. Herman said, "You guys nearly missed a great show," as he pulled out a bag and handed it to me. I looked inside and found a variety of sex toys and lubricants. "Now you can finish what you were doing," Herman said as he led our little group to his cabin.

The men got comfortable in anticipation of my performance. Rob's cock started to expand as I reached into the bag and pulled out a dildo. It was about fourteen inches long and shaped like a cock, with a large head and thick shaft. I lay back on the bed and positioned myself so they could see my pussy as I began to play. I started to spread my lips apart, but my pussy was sticky from the fucking Herman had given me so I had to slide my finger along the crease in order to expose my clit. As I lightly flicked at my clit, I looked at the men and saw their cocks swelling in appreciation. I grabbed the dildo and rubbed it on my pussy until it was slippery with juice, then slowly inserted the big head. At first it seemed as if it wouldn't fit, but my pussy gradually opened wider until I could slide half of it in with each stroke. My clit was totally exposed now, and with each thrust of the dildo my body tensed with ecstasy. Herman reached over and flicked a switch, which turned on the vibrator inside the dildo. I thought I would pass out as I came over and over again. I continued to pump it until I reached a level of excitement I had never known before. I was totally out of control, and I found myself begging them to fuck me. Herman removed the dildo and rammed his huge cock into my cunt.

The pleasure was so intense I couldn't help but scream. Herman came with a shout and pulled out as I continued to twitch. Lou immediately took his place and filled me with his cock in one thrust. It felt so good to have another hot, throbbing cock inside me that I thrust up against him so he could plunge even deeper into me. He obliged by fucking me harder and harder. I was starting to come again when he pulled out. Herman pulled me on top of him and took another turn pounding my pussy. As I rode him I felt my juices running down my thighs. The squishy sounds of sex filled the cabin. He played with my tits as I bounced on top of him. Suddenly Herman rolled me over and positioned me on my hands and knees. After he had reinserted his huge shaft inside me, Rob knelt in front of me so I could lick and suck him.

Rob and Herman stopped moving for a moment. Then they began to move in rhythm—Herman steadily fucking my cunt and Rob fucking my mouth. It was the most intense feeling

I have ever had. I felt another orgasm building, and panted and bucked as I went over the edge. They came as well and I felt rivers of come fill my body.

After they pulled out, Rob came over with a towel and helped me clean up. As he tenderly wiped me off, he leaned over and gave me a long, slow lick from head to toe. Even though I was exhausted, the feel of his tongue made my juices flow again. I gasped in pleasure at his touch, and was very disappointed when he stopped and went on deck with the others. I must have fallen asleep after that, because the next thing I knew I heard different voices outside. I looked at the clock and found that it was nine-thirty at night.

I looked out the window and saw that we had hooked up with another boat. There seemed to be a wild party going on. Lou was on the other boat smoking a joint, and Herman was calling for his "grog" like a pirate. I quickly went up to join the party.

I was greeted with a loud cheer. Herman said he figured I was asleep for the night. He introduced me to the crew of the other boat, and I was pleased to see that they were as young and good-looking as my friends. I got a bit apprehensive when I realized that I was the only woman, but my nervousness disappeared after a drink.

I sat up on the deck with Lou and a man from the other boat named Jim. While we and shared a joint, Lou rubbed my shoulders. Jim said, "I could use a little of that," so he sat down between my legs and I massaged his shoulders and upper back. Lou began to get a bit playful, squeezing my nipples and stroking the sides of my breasts. It felt good, but I kept silent because I didn't want Jim to know what was happening. When Lou tried to pull my shirt off I had to raise my arms, so Jim he turned around to see why I stopped his massage. He received a bird's-eye view of my big breasts spilling out of my bikini top. He turned back around without saying a word, and I resumed working on his muscular shoulders while Lou resumed working on my tits.

I felt Lou untie my top, then felt his nimble fingers all over my naked breasts. As he touched me I got more and more turned on. Unconsciously my hands slid around Jim's body to feel his muscular chest. I knew he was enjoying it because his breathing quickened, and he had to change his position to create more room for his growing cock. Lou had taken his cock out of his shorts and was slowly dry-humping me from behind with long, slow strokes. I reached between Jim's legs and grabbed his cock.

He gasped when I touched the large, swollen head that was protruding from the waistband of his shorts. I could feel the sticky pre-come oozing from his slit as I squeezed his thick shaft. I panted, "Let me see it," so he quickly turned around and spread his legs for me. I pulled his shorts down and squealed with pleasure as his heavy cock sprang into view. I started to suck on him, and he groaned loudly as I slid my mouth up and down his shaft. Lou took advantage of this position and slid his cock into me doggie-style. Jim didn't last very long. After only a few minutes he stiffened and shot his load down my throat. He thanked me and walked away, leaving me with Lou's cock still thrusting into my swollen pussy and his hands cupping my tits.

Jim must have told his shipmates about what happened, because it wasn't long before I looked up to see two more guys from the other boat standing before me with their hard cocks in their hands. I ended up sucking both of them to orgasm before Lou finally came.

Lou and I went to the back of the boat to find Herman and Adam, the captain of the other boat, waiting for us. Adam asked if I'd like a tour of his boat, and as we carefully walked over and went down to his cabin, I knew exactly what he wanted. His boat was larger than Herman's, and his cabin was outfitted with a stereo system and a bar. He made me a drink, then we sat down on the edge of the bed and talked. His eyes continually dropped down to my tits and the hard nipples jutting through my shirt. When he'd look back at me I returned the favor by looking directly at his crotch and his growing bulge. Suddenly he reached up and lightly flicked one nipple, then the other, which sent shocks to my clit. He pushed me back on the bed, pulled my shirt up and sucked my nipples. After a few minutes he stood up and pulled off his shorts.

Adam's cock was hard, thick and hot. I pulled him between my legs and guided his missile into my pussy. I couldn't believe how easy it had become for me to fuck another man. Just the sight of a hard cock and I was ready. Adam pumped me with fast, hard strokes until he came. He pulled out immediately, only to be replaced by Jim, then George and Eric (the two men I had blown earlier). I lost count of how many times each one entered me and how many times I came. The evening was a blur. Finally Herman came aboard and carried me back to his boat.

I fell asleep in Herman's cabin and didn't wake up until we were nearly home. The morning was bright and beautiful, and while my body was tired, my pussy still oozed and tingled.

My husband met me at the dock and I could tell right away that he knew what had happened. I introduced him to Herman and the guys, then all of us headed for a pub to celebrate our successful voyage. But that's another story.

A Girl Called Spike

When I was twenty, I used to ride with a gang of bikers. We had a ball, partying every night until the sun rose. Biker parties are the best—there's always plenty of wild chicks running around.

I'm not a bad-looking man, but I am honest enough to admit that I'm not every chick's fantasy come to life either. I'm five foot seven, weigh almost two hundred pounds, have brown hair and brown eyes. I rode a Harley back then and, believe me, no woman ever came between me and my bike.

Anyway, at one party I was introduced to a woman named Jeannie. Jeannie, at the time, was thirty-one and built like a goddess. She had shoulder-length blonde hair, green eyes and weighed about one hundred twenty pounds. She was only five feet tall. Everybody called her Spike for some reason.

After someone introduced us, she stuck to me like glue. I didn't mind. She was hot.

Later that night Jeannie and I, along with a couple of friends, decided to head out to a concert. As the night wore on, I became quite attached to Jeannie. We started talking as if we were old friends, even though we had known each other only a short while. The concert ended and we all got ready to split. I kissed her, and we promised to meet at an upcoming party.

That Friday night, when I arrived at Stinkin' Steve's house for the party, I was surprised to find that there were about forty guys and only six women there. Jeannie was one of them. It took all of ten seconds before the two of us were seriously making out.

The party got into swing real quick. Beer flowed like water. We also had Jack Daniel's and Wild Turkey. Nice, thick joints were passed around.

Jeannie and I were sitting on the small couch near the corner, and we were getting friendly. I noticed at that time that all the other women were nowhere to be found. I paid no attention since I had Jeannie.

At about six that night, Jeannie told me to follow her. We headed toward one of the back bedrooms. While we were on our way, we could hear loud moaning coming from another bedroom. We looked in and saw the three women and a group of guys going at it like there was no tomorrow. We watched for a while and received quite a sight, but soon grew more interested in each other.

I have to tell you, this woman was a fireball of passion. Now, I'm no John Holmes, as I've stated earlier, but I think I am more than able to please a woman. As soon as we were behind the closed door, Jeannie was on the floor fighting to remove my clothes. All I could do was sit back and enjoy. She quickly had my cock so far down her throat, I was amazed. While working on my cock, she slipped out of her top. I don't think it took her more than one minute to get fully undressed.

I was still dressed, with my cock hanging out of my fly. I told her to stop for a second so that I could get out of the rest of my clothes.

We got into a 69. I must say, she had one of the sweetest

cunts I have ever tasted. She worked on me for a good twenty minutes before allowing me to come. And when I did, she shoved my cock all the way down her throat so she could get every drop.

She was smiling after that. I pulled her down onto her back, crawled on top and went to work sucking her cunt. She started moaning and telling me to fuck her already. Well, I believe in making a woman happy, so I quickly agreed. I got on top and slid my cock into her as slowly as possible. I didn't think she would ever stop coming. Her legs shot up over my shoulders. Once she had settled down I used long, slow strokes.

We must have been screwing for a solid hour before I could feel my orgasm approaching. I slowed down so that she could catch up to me. It was great when we exploded together.

It seemed only a few minutes had passed before she grabbed my cock and pulled me up onto her chest. She placed my cock between her tits. I began thrusting back and forth. Jeannie sucked the tip of my cock. She really enjoyed getting tit-fucked. When I finally came in her mouth, it was great! Jeannie thought so too, since she licked my cock clean.

We went back and joined everyone else. Soon the party really got going. Everybody got fucked up and ripped their clothes off. It was like an indoor nudist camp. Then Jeannie told me she was going to the bathroom.

About forty-five minutes went by. I started getting head from this one chick, so I didn't notice time slip by. Then someone called to me from one of the bedrooms. When I stepped into the bedroom, I got a real shock. There was my Jeannie, on the bed with legs stretched back so that her ankles were on her shoulders. She was fucking herself with a thick black dildo. When she realized how many guys were in the bedroom watching her, she told us to gather around the bed. She got on all fours, without removing the dildo, and started sucking and licking our cocks one at a time.

I don't think there was a limp cock in the house. Everybody wanted Jeannie. So without further delay, I reached down and pulled the dildo from her cunt. She moaned loudly. While one guy was getting his stick licked, I crawled up behind her and slid into a cunt that was so hot I thought my cock was going to burn off. I didn't want to come just then, so I pulled out and worked my cockhead up and down her slit to get her even hotter. I spit on my cock and slowly worked it back in. She was quite tight for a woman who seemed to enjoy fucking so much.

As I slowly stroked in and out of her, she pulled her lips away from the cock she was sucking. Her mouth was full of come, as the guy had orgasmed between her lips. After swallowing the guy's load, she turned her head and told me to take my time because she wanted me to last the entire ride.

She hung her head over the edge of the bed and resumed sucking cock as if she was born to it. While she was doing this, one of the other guys got on her and fucked her tits. She held them together to help him. All that time I was fucking her cunt like a battering ram. I must have been on the verge of coming about five different times, but each time I stopped and waited for the approaching orgasm to melt away.

So, there I was, fucking sweet Jeannie's pussy and watching the action happening around me. She had a cock in her mouth and one between her tits. When the guy fucking her mouth was about to explode, she yanked him out and jerked him off, adding his load onto her chest. It was a sight to see!

She finally took the last cock between her lips. It didn't take him more than five minutes to come. When she realized she'd finished them all, she told them to leave the room so she could be alone with me. I was pleasantly surprised, to say the least!

When they were all gone, she got on her hands and knees and told me to keep right on fucking her. While I did that, Jeannie grabbed the Wild Turkey and started licking the neck of the bottle. I reached around and played with her tits. I love nothing more than a set of large, firm tits. Her tits met all the requirements, with nipples as hard as rocks. It was then I realized why they called her Spike. It was because her nipples were like spikes.

I was reaching another orgasm. Jeannie started whimpering as I shot my load. When I was spent, I pulled out. Jeannie took my cock in her mouth and sucked it back to life. When I finally got hard again, I told her to sit on my cock and ride me. She did so, riding me as if she were a jockey. At one point she leaped so high my wet cock flopped out. Then she leaned over and put her tits right in my face and told me to suck her nipples. She told me to let her know when I was going to come, because she wanted it in her mouth.

When we finished, it took us twenty minutes to clean up in the shower. I'm glad I met Jeannie. To this day she and I are happy together. She doesn't mess around as much as she used to, but when she wants to, I allow it. There is nothing like a big-titted woman to show a man what fucking is all about. Whoever said more than a mouthful is a waste didn't know what he was talking about.

More Than a Mouthful

I have always been excited by women with large breasts. My wife Angie keeps me more than happy in this department.

Angie's best friend is Julia. They shared a room back when they were in college. Julia has breasts of truly astounding proportions. She never dated much as far as I could tell. The thought of those tits not giving or receiving pleasure truly disappointed me.

Julia and I used to have fairly explicit discussions about sex and masturbation. I never thought I'd ever get to enjoy her delights.

About a year after we graduated from college, Julia came to town to see a play with us. To avoid the late-night drive home, she asked if she could spend the evening with us. We, of course, agreed.

After spending an enjoyable evening at the theater, we went back to the house. My wife was working the night shift that week, so she changed clothes and left. Julia and I were alone as we prepared to retire.

I realized that this was my big chance. I got out the vibrator I'd given my wife last Christmas and went into the living room. Julia, clad in only a long flannel shirt, was lounging on the couch writing in her diary.

"Remember those discussions we had in college, when you were wondering whether it was okay to masturbate?" I asked her.

"Yes," she said.

"Do you masturbate?"

"Oh, yes. It's quite enjoyable, to say the least."

"Glad to hear you say that. May I ask what you've used?" As I said, our previous discussions were pretty straightforward, so even this frank question didn't faze her in the slightest.

"Not too much. I usually just use my fingers," she casually replied.

"Ever try a vibrator?"

Julia's eyebrows raised. I could see she was interested. Then she asked, "Why? Do you have one?"

"Funny you should ask . . ." I sat beside her on the couch and let her examine the toy for a little while. Then I showed her how to turn it on.

"It can be used on any part of the body," I remarked. I pressed it against the side of one of her breasts and gently ran it up and down. Even through the flannel shirt it stimulated her. She tensed and drew back. As calmly as I could, I told her to relax and allow the demonstration to give her the full effect. She thought a minute, then shrugged. She rested her head back on the couch and let me continue. Soon I was caressing her nipples with the vibrator's golden tip. I was dying to pull her shirt off so that I could finally see those huge white globes of quivering flesh.

Julia immensely enjoyed what I was doing to her. I put my hand on her knee and tried to pull her legs apart. She tensed up again. It took a little coaxing and reassuring, but I was finally able to convince her that there was nothing wrong with what we were doing, that it was simply good, clean fun between good friends. She spread her legs, and I ran the buzzing vibrator along her inner thighs. I worked my way upward and began to rub her pussy through her panties.

By now Julia was enjoying herself without reservation. She placed her hand over mine and helped guide the vibrator. I knew I had it made. I reached up with my free hand and squeezed her large, heaving breasts. I held the firm flesh through her shirt and bra and rolled her nipples between my fingers. When I suggested she get comfortable so we could do the job right, she raised her hips and pulled her panties off. I unbuttoned her shirt and helped her off with it. From behind her, I undid the hooks that held her bra tight, then slowly lifted the cups off the huge twin globes.

I watched in awe as her giant white tits flopped down onto her tummy, then rolled off to each side of her chest as she lay down on the couch. I picked up the vibrator again, wet it in my mouth and placed it on her bare pussy. She gasped and arched her back at the contact. I worked the vibrator around the opening of her pussy for a while, occasionally touching her clitoris. Finally I pushed the tool inside her. She let out a soft, low moan, then placed her hand over mine and helped me bury it inside her to the hilt.

Then she took over, slowly moving the vibrator in and out of her hungry pussy. I stroked her thighs briefly, then concentrated on those huge, delicious breasts that had enchanted me for so many years.

Julia continued working on herself with the vibrator while I buried my face between her tits, luxuriating in the feeling of having the soft, smooth flesh press against each side of my face.

All this time she continued to move the vibrator in and out of her pussy. She was working her way toward one monster of an orgasm. When her climax hit, she let out a scream and jammed the vibrator deep into her cunt. I pressed my fingers deep into the soft flesh of her hot tits. As her spasms subsided,

I relaxed my grip and started tenderly kneading and stroking her tits. She turned the vibrator off and slowly pulled it out. She opened her eyes, looked at me and said, "Wow. What a kick. Thanks."

"I thought you'd like it. Now, while you're recovering, I have another question for you. Have you ever watched a man masturbate?"

My cock felt like it was about to burst. My balls felt swollen and heavy. I just had to get off somehow.

"No, but I've always wanted to watch a man jerk off," Julia said thoughtfully. "If you feel like demonstrating, go right ahead."

I quickly shed my pajamas and stretched out on the floor. I reached down, stroked my hard prick with one hand and rubbed my balls with the other. I kept my eyes on Julia's plump, naked body, explaining that I'd never jerked off in front of a woman before. My tempo gradually increased. Julia started fingering her clit and rubbing her big tits while intently watching me jerk off.

She sat down beside me. I moved my head onto her lap. While I continued my demonstration, I stroked, squeezed and nibbled her tits, which were hanging down onto my face. Julia pitched in by rubbing my chest and thighs while continuing to watch my hand pumping away.

As my orgasm approached, I slowed my tempo and warned Julia to watch. The closer I got, the slower I stroked. Soon I had the strongest orgasm I'd ever experienced. Big spurts of come shot three feet into the air, landing on my stomach and chest. A few drops even splattered Julia's breasts. She curiously lifted each breast and licked the drops. I couldn't tell from her expression whether or not she liked the taste.

I got up and started to pull my clothes on.

"It certainly has been an enjoyable, educational evening," she said. "Mind if I keep the vibrator?"

After what we'd just been through, how could I refuse? I invited her to spend the night with me.

I set the alarm to go off an hour before my wife returned from work. That would leave Julia plenty of time to return to the couch. We settled down to sleep. She lay with her back to me. I gently cupped her breasts.

I bought a new vibrator the next day, before my wife had a chance to notice her old one was missing. To this day, I wonder what Julia ended up writing in her diary that night.

The Widow Maker

Last night a very strange yet touching thing happened to me. I boarded a flight at O'Hare Airport in Chicago on my way to a business trip in San Francisco. Next to me, in the window seat, was an attractive older woman who, I later learned, was sixty-one years old. I have always found women of all ages attractive. I enjoy checking out ladies in their fifties just as much as those who, like me, are in their twenties. I noticed that she had a trim figure, a well-endowed chest and wonderful legs—and she was dressed entirely in black. I started to read a book, but heard her crying. So I put my book down and asked what was wrong.

The woman apologized for distracting me and said she couldn't help crying. She introduced herself as Arlene and went on to explain that her husband had just died after a long bout with cancer. She was returning from burying him at his family's plot in New York. I encouraged her to talk, thinking that this might make her feel better, and by the time we began our descent into San Francisco, Arlene and I were chatting like old friends.

I noticed that she had slipped her shoes off. To someone with a foot fetish, such as me, it resulted in an instant erection.

The sight of this widow's shapely feet and well-manicured toes encased in sheer, black hose was driving me wild.

By the time we landed I was quite heated up. Arlene and I deplaned with the rest of the passengers and picked up our luggage. She told me she couldn't bear to spend that first night at home without her husband, so I suggested she get a room in the hotel where I was staying. She thought it was a good idea, and we took a cab there together.

Unfortunately, upon arriving we learned that the hotel was booked up. The desk clerk called around, but all the area hotels were full due to a convention. I offered Arlene my room and told her I'd sleep in the lobby. She thanked me, but said she would only accept if I stayed in the room. I insisted that she take the bed, and I offered to sleep on the floor. She agreed to go upstairs and said, "We'll settle the sleeping arrangements later."

We took turns showering. I came out of the bathroom wrapped in a towel. Arlene was making up a bed for herself on the floor. My cock stiffened at the sight of her in a short robe, cut well above the knee. A vision of her lovely legs wrapped around my waist flashed through my mind.

Arlene and I haggled some more over who would sleep where, until I finally convinced her to take the bed. She did so, and I curled up on the floor. Once under the blanket, I pulled off my towel and tried to get comfortable. I watched Arlene walk to the bed and turn out the light. The drapes weren't fully closed, and thanks to the light coming into the room I caught a glimpse of Arlene as she untied her robe and let it drop to the floor. I was surprised to see that she, too, was naked! With wide eyes I watched her firm ass and legs as she pulled down the blankets. As she eased herself between the sheets, I got a good look at her full, mature breasts. I drifted off to sleep and was soon having erotic dreams involving the widow sleeping naked only a few feet from me.

Sometime during the night I awoke and stumbled to the bathroom to relieve myself. Still half asleep, I automatically went to the bed and started to pull back the sheets to get in. I saw Arlene's sleeping form in the bed and suddenly remembered the circumstances. I was about to drop the sheets and return to my bed on the floor when Arlene muttered in her sleep, "Ted, stop standing there and get into bed. You're making me cold." Ted, as I recalled from our conversation on the plane, was her deceased husband.

Arlene then reached out, grabbed me by the arm and pulled me into the bed. I settled down between the sheets, determined to slip out as soon as she was fully asleep again. However, Arlene prevented my escape by rolling into my arms with her head on my chest and one leg wrapped around mine.

I lay there, awake, for about twenty minutes. With each passing second my erection grew more insistent as I felt Arlene's breasts pressing into my side and chest. Her cunt hair tickled my thigh each time she shifted her position. My dick grew so stiff and tall that I soon felt it touch Arlene's hand. I was speechless when her hand slipped off her thigh and curled around my cock!

Arlene began to stroke my aching cock and muttered in a sleepy voice, "I see you brought me a present, Ted. I've missed it and boy, do I need it." I was convinced that Arlene was still asleep and thought I was her dead husband Ted. I was debating what to do, when she abruptly threw off the covers and rose to her hands and knees. Arlene raised her left leg, eased it over my hips and leaned forward to give me a passion-filled kiss. I felt her position my cock at the entrance to her pussy as she probed my tonsils with her tongue. I noted that throughout all of this, her eyes were still closed.

After several moments of kissing, the head of my cock began to pry her warm pussy lips apart. I watched as her eyelids slowly started to rise. The shock and surprise on her face was a sight I will always remember. She said, "You're not Ted!" but that didn't seem to change her mind about wanting to get fucked. She wiggled her hips from side to side, slowly working her way down my fat, hard rod. I still wasn't sure if she was really surprised to see me or if this was all just some fantasy she needed to act out, but it couldn't have mattered less. The fiery grip of Arlene's cunt took hold of my tool and sucked it all the way in.

And then nature took over. Arlene's hips moved instinctively and with the expertise of a woman who'd been riding cock all her life. My hips automatically began moving with hers. Arlene's mouthing of such words as "Yes, yes, it feels so good" soon gave way to animal grunts and cries of, "That's it, give me that dick. Give it hard!"

In between her groans and gasps, Arlene told me it had been two years since she'd had sex. Apparently her husband had been too sick to fuck her for a long time, and she'd been so busy looking after him she didn't have time to take care of her own sexual needs.

Arlene's hips were moving so fast they were a blur, and she soon climaxed in a series of orgasms that released two years of pent-up frustration. My cock, tormented for a mere six or seven hours by the presence of this shapely widow, soon demanded its own release. "Come inside me, honey," Arlene urged. "I want to feel your load." I was soon blasting a torrent of thick love-milk deep into her long-neglected pussy.

Arlene collapsed into my arms and cried tears of happiness and joy at her sexual release. If she felt any remorse at being in bed with a stranger only a few days after her husband's death, it soon passed, for in just a few minutes she was kissing her way down my chest and stomach to my cock.

Arlene licked up the juices that were still clinging to my

cock, then took me into her mouth. Her bobbing head soon had me erect and ready for action once more. I rolled her over and eased my cock into her waiting snatch. This time she was wet and waiting for me.

My mouth found her breasts, and I sucked her big, erect nipples deep into my mouth. With her legs wrapped tightly around my waist, I rammed my cock deep into her cunt with all my strength. Arlene came several times, crying out for more as I hammered away. I kept changing the depth and pace of my strokes to maximize her pleasure and to prolong my own coming.

When I was close to orgasm again, I pulled out of Arlene's cunt and placed my throbbing cock between her breasts. I began to pump in and out between the two mounds of heavenly flesh. Arlene had raised her head and was licking the tip of my cock with each stroke. Knowing I was on the edge, I released Arlene's breasts and placed my cock in her mouth. It only took a couple of in-and-out thrusts for me to pump a load of semen into her hot mouth and down her throat.

We finally fell off to sleep. The next morning, before checking out, I screwed Arlene doggie-style on the floor and shot my come all over the bed. After I'd confided to her that I was a foot fetishist, Arlene put on her black nylons and jerked me off with her feet. I shot my final load all over those sheer stockings, which she then gave to me as a souvenir of our brief time together.

What do Americans love almost as much as sex? Talking about it. Here, as told in their own, uninhibited words, is the state of the union between men and women today, in all its inventive, eccentric, energetic variety. The sex is unbelievable . . . and every word is true!

- [ ] **THE PENTHOUSE LETTERS**
  (0-446-35778-2, $5.99 USA) ($6.99 Can.)
- [ ] **MORE LETTERS FROM PENTHOUSE**
  (0-446-34515-6, $5.99 USA) ($6.99 Can.)
- [ ] **LETTERS TO PENTHOUSE III**
  (0-446-36296-4, $5.99 USA) ($6.99 Can.)
- [ ] **LETTERS TO PENTHOUSE IV**
  (0-446-60056-4, $5.99 USA) ($6.99 Can.)
- [ ] **LETTERS TO PENTHOUSE V**
  (0-446-60195-0, $5.99 USA) ($6.99 Can.)
- [ ] **LETTERS TO PENTHOUSE VI**
  (0-446-60196-9, $5.99 USA) ($6.99 Can.)
- [ ] **EROTICA FROM PENTHOUSE**
  (0-446-34517-2, $5.99 USA) ($6.99 Can.)
- [ ] **EROTICA FROM PENTHOUSE III**
  (0-446-60057-1, $5.99 USA) ($6.99 Can.)
- [ ] **MORE EROTICA FROM PENTHOUSE**
  (0-446-36297-2, $5.99 USA) ($6.99 Can.)

Available at a bookstore near you from
Warner Books.